COVEN COVE

BloodLust

David Clark

1

"I thought I was going to join Lisa in class." I looked around the empty classroom that seemed like it was right out of a gothic horror movie.

"Not all dark magic is the same. Different witch. Different magic. Different class," replied Mr. Demius. "We need to find out what kind of witch you are." He said while putting away several large leather-bound books. By the looks of the wear on their covers, these were old, which didn't surprise me, considering what he taught.

"Mrs. Tenderschott already did that."

"Um, yes. Her crystals," he mocked. "I am talking about true magic. Come up here to the front of the class." He motioned for me to walk down the stone steps. I half expected to find some cherubs up on the walls; maybe perched over one of his many stone archways, but there weren't any. Good! It was just us, and six empty tables. Three on each side of the central stairs. At the front, the desk that I assumed Mr. Demius used during class resembled an altar, but not from any religion I recognized. Dark wood, much like the ritual room, and old iron accents.

"Let us dispense with the pop culture magic that is taught down the hall. There is a lot more to this than throwing fire, making things grow, and pushing things around. You come from a time when magic was different. It was truly special. I need to see how much of it you were introduced to." With a wave of his hand, five flaming symbols appeared in front of my face. "Miss Dubois, do you recognize any of those?"

I studied the symbols closely. Each burned deep inside me with a familiarity that was hard to shake. I just couldn't place them. Had I seen them in Mrs. Saxon's class, or maybe in some of my reading that I had done under Edward's supervision? Something I hadn't told Mrs. Saxon about yet, though I doubt she would mind someone making use of the library. At least somebody was. The more comfortable I became, the more I wanted to stretch my wings. I walked closer and looked at each symbol one at a time. That was when it hit me out of nowhere. A single memory of my mother and the same five symbols floating in the air with flames radiating out from them. My mouth echoed her words. "The five elements of the world."

"Almost," he replied with a bit of a surprise, but it still came out as disappointed.

"Wait!" I exclaimed as my head attempted to process the memory and the lesson she gave me. Before I answered, the door opened and in walked Master Benjamin Thomas and one of the several Mr. Demius look-a-likes from the council; dark clothes, black stringy hair, and all. Even down to the way he carried himself when he walked. Each step was careful and deliberate, while leaning slightly back to ensure he was always looking down his nose at everything and everyone. The original didn't seem too surprised by the interruption as he reached to greet Master Thomas.

"Larissa, good to see you." He joined me in front of the symbols.

"Good to see you too, Master Thomas." I still couldn't make myself call him by his first name only. It had nothing to do with age, which I was his senior. It was respect for his position in our world. Behind the symbols, the two dark lords were sharing a less than friendly greeting.

"I didn't tell Leonard I was bringing him," Master Thomas leaned over and whispered to me. "They have a bit of ah, um, a history."

I could tell, but didn't ask what it was. I was too busy absorbing the news that our own dark lord's name was Leonard.

"I didn't know you were coming today."

"I wouldn't miss this for the world. So, do you know what these symbols are?" He asked, and the other two dark figures joined us on the floor in front of the symbols.

"The five elements of the magic world," I responded, repeating the words my mother said in my memory.

"I knew it," Master Thomas celebrated with a clap of his hand. "She remembers."

"Who showed these to you?" Mr. Demius asked.

"My mother."

"That would make sense," added our guest. "Much of that area was stuck in the old ways until just recently. The more important question, does she know what they mean? And I don't mean the traditional meanings. I mean the magical meanings."

All three sets of eyes focused right on me. The only things missing were a spotlight and goofy game-show music with a clock ticking in the background. I tried to ignore them, but couldn't ignore the urge to look back over my shoulder at them from time to time. In between glances, I studied the symbols, hoping to hear my mother's voice cutting through the silence in my head. Either from her finding some way to talk to me from the great beyond, or from a memory.

The first symbol was a triangle with a line across the middle of it. I knew this one. I was certain of it. It was right there on the tip of my tongue, and it didn't appear I was going to get any help from my mother on this one. The way I thought about it, half the work in remembering what this was had already happened. I remembered the symbols and what my mother called them. There wasn't any doubt in my head that she covered a few of them in that same session. Now if only I could recall that memory. I could see us standing there in the parlor. Well, she was standing, and I was sitting on the French settee we had. I loved napping on that when I was small enough to fit. Not because of the settee, but because of the breezes that came in through the windows behind it. My mother displayed the symbols in the air much like Mr. Demius had, but there were more, a lot more. What did we do after she showed them to me? She would have gone through them one by one, wouldn't she? Like any teacher. They don't just show you the alphabet and say go. They show it to you and then start with the first letter. What was first? Then, again, it hit me. This time it wasn't her voice, it was my own. "This is fire." I looked back for confirmation and saw three hopeful faces. I was at least partially right.

"What can we use it for?" prompted Mr. Demius.

I finally understood what they were after. Now if only I could remember what we used each item for. I turned my attention back to the symbol for fire. Of course, it was fire, but that symbol was not used to create fire; thank you chapter one of Mrs. Saxon's book of spells. There had to be a deeper meaning, a more magical meaning.

"Change?" I answered, remembering her words as she explained it.

"Bingo!" Master Thomas exclaimed with another clap of his hands. "Larissa, fire is the agent and energy for change. It can both destroy and create."

"Did your mother tell you this?" our guest queried.

"Sorry Larissa. You must excuse my manners," interjected Master Thomas before I could answer. "I forgot to introduce you to Mr. Theodore Nevers. Our master of the dark world and resident geek of everything old."

"A pleasure to meet you, Larissa," Mr. Nevers said. He never attempted to reach forward and still kept his distance. A common reaction the first time anyone met me.

"Nice to meet you, and yes, I remember her telling me that, but that is about all, I think," I answered, unsure. The search was happening behind my eyes, and so far was coming up with lots of blanks with only a few flashes of information.

"I am willing to bet she showed you more. You just don't remember, yet," Master Thomas stated while appearing to do a little celebratory dance. "Let's see if we can get it out of you."

I wasn't in the mood for anyone to go poking around in my head. Since my last trip with Miss Roberts, no one had. My thoughts had been my thoughts, and I liked it that way.

"I want you to picture that symbol in your head, feel it, and let it be one with you, all while you imagine standing on a patch of green grass," instructed Master Thomas. I must have looked at him like he had two heads by the way he returned my look. "Trust me," he encouraged.

"All right," I agreed, though I was still a little unsure. I closed my eyes and tried exactly what he said. I imagined it just as he told me to. The fire left the symbol, and it drew itself over and over in my head. Faster and faster. It was hard to focus on the second part of his instructions while the symbol danced in and out of existence right in front of me. I had to force myself to think of standing on green grass. That was when the flash happened in my head, and I heard a loud whoosh around me causing my eyes to spring open just in time to see a line of fire expanding out from me, leaving behind it a layer of green grass on the floor.

I bent down to touch it and pulled on it. A few moist green blades broke free in my hands, blade, root, dirt, and all. I let it sit on my open palm while I asked. "Is it real?" I had to be sure.

"Yes, it is real," answered a smiling Master Thomas.

Mr. Demius bent down in front of me and yanked at a larger section until it broke free. He lifted it up, showing me the stone floor below. Even he appeared to smile as he displayed this for me to see.

This was something. Something new and extraordinary, but then I remembered. I had done this before, once, with my mother. While I tried to remember what it was I created, I watched as Mr. Demius stood up with closed eyes, and a flash of fire rolled down him and expanded out, removing the grass and leaving the stone floor clean.

"It can also destroy just as easy," he said, just as I remembered what it was.

I held out both hands, and before I could consider if this was wise or not, I thought of the symbol again, and then what my nine-year-old self wanted almost a hundred years ago. There was a similar flash, and I didn't need to open my eyes to know it worked. I felt its webbed feet on the palms of my hands, and the fluffy fuzz of a baby duck tickled my fingers.

I smiled when I opened my eyes, and resisted saying, "Ta-da." The faces staring back at me were filled with terror, and I checked the duck to make sure I didn't create some demonic creature instead. Who knew if my other dark side would have any effects?

"Larissa, you can create life?" Mr. Demius asked, his voice quavered.

"Did I do something wrong?" I panicked. Based on the faces that stared back at me, I felt I had. Like I had broken some rule or now I was the one with two heads.

"No," Master Thomas replied hastily, though his expression and tone were not convincing. He stepped forward and looked at the duck. "May I?" I nodded, and he took the duck from my hands.

"Larissa," he said breathlessly, while one hand held the duckling, and the other caressed its fuzz. He was like a boy on Christmas morning. "You need to understand, what you did is something that... is extraordinary." he passed the duck to Mr. Demius, "It's not something many can do."

"Any," interjected Mr. Nevers.

"I have heard stories of others," Master Thomas said, addressing his fellow council member. "There have been, and are others, and one was your mother. I read a few accounts of it when I was looking into your background to understand Mrs. Wintercrest's interest. I had no idea it would have passed down. Did she teach you how to do that?"

"Sort of," I said, remembering more and more every moment. "She taught me about that power of creation, and I tried it over and over, challenging myself each time." When that part of my mind remembered the rest of the memory from my nine-year-old self, I saw my mother's reaction and shuddered. "Oh god!"

"She was not pleased when you did it before, was she?" asked Master Thomas.

"No, she was angry. One of the few times she ever was angry with me." I bit my lip as I remembered why and looked at the cute innocent duck in Mr. Nevers' hands and knew the cost.

"Do you understand why?" Mr. Demius asked.

"To create a life, you have to take a life." I answered, my voice shook remembering the lesson my mother taught me.

"That's right," stated Master Thomas. "The universe has a balance, and not even witches can change that balance."

"Nothing to worry about, dear child," Mr. Demius said. He spun his hand around quickly and opened a portal to a pond that was out in a sunny meadow. He stepped through and put the little duckling down. "He will flourish here with his brothers." Just as he said that the duck waddled down to the water and swam across the surface and joined a group of six others. My last view of it before the portal closed was the adult duck grooming its fuzz. "We need to see what else you know, so we can properly train you on how to deal with these gifts. How about these?" He wiped his hand across the air, erasing the four flaming symbols, and replacing them with two of his own.

I walked forward to the first one. It was one I had seen recently, in the runes Mrs. Saxon put on the doors to keep Jean St. Claire from getting in. My finger pointed at it and traced its shape. "The sun," I started, and then corrected myself. "The solar cross. That is for protection."

"Good," cheered Master Thomas. "Do you know how to use it?"

"Yes, it can be used in two different ways. Written in runes," which I didn't really know before now, but felt it was safe to make the assumption since I recognized it in the runes Mrs. Saxon had written on the floor of the ritual room, and around the doors to try to keep Reginald out. Its usage in spells was what I was surer about. My mother had taught me that, though I never really used it for protection per se, but I did use it once to keep Charles Snyder out of my room when he made me mad when I was ten. A move he complained about to his mother. If I remembered correctly, my mother just smiled.

"That's right," Mr. Nevers said, sounding surprised. "How about the other symbol?"

2

After an afternoon and early evening of being quizzed on symbol after symbol, my brain was exhausted. Which didn't make me good company for Nathan and Amy during our nightly story time. It was Mrs. Saxon's one concession to Nathan's house arrest, which was what we called his grounding. She felt the nightly event was important to Amy, and she wasn't going to punish her because we were, as she called it, stupid and irresponsible. There was also a remark that it could be good for us too. She couldn't have been more right. It refreshed me, and that was something I was going to need for a while.

At the end of my session with Mr. Demius, Mr. Nevers, and Master Thomas, I was told there was much I was aware of, but my knowledge stopped there and lacked the depth on each topic that I would need, and they would need to correct that. Mr. Demius told me that would require a lot of extra work on top of my existing classes. While I didn't really like the thought of the extra work, there were two benefits that I couldn't ignore. I needed the work to recover what I knew and finish the teaching my mother had started, and, with Nathan grounded for who knows how long, I found myself with an abundance of free time on my hands. Having something to fill that wouldn't be bad.

By the time I rejoined the others up on the deck, the music was going, and Brad, Mike, and Jeremy were in the middle of what appeared to be a very distracted game of poker. From what I could see, all three of them had losing hands, yet none of them took any cards. I doubted if any of them had even looked at their hands. Their heads, and those of everyone else up on the deck, were craned to look at the other end of the deck. I followed their gaze and saw Mr. Bolden sitting down there with someone else. Whoever it was had their back to us and wore a black hoodie. Mr. Bolden was talking, but whoever it was, wasn't responding.

"So, is that our new visitor?" I asked as I sat down between Apryl and Jennifer.

"Yep," Apryl said, but her head never turned in my direction.

Jennifer was reading a magazine, and was the only one that seemed to ignore what was going on at the other end of the deck. "Yep, that's him. His name is Clayton Lindsey. He is struggling, but Kevin will bring him around. He always has," she said with a smile. "Sometimes it just takes a while. It's different for everyone. Sometimes it is easier to bring them around when they have been a vampire longer, and other times it isn't because they are set in their ways. Sometimes those that have just turned are easier because they are confused and looking for guidance, but then you also have those that are still raw with anger and animalistic instinct; It just depends on the person. This one appears to still be in that raw, angry state."

"So, that is what I heard last night?"

"Yes. He put up quite a fight. Kevin hasn't broken him yet, but at least Clayton knows he can't beat him. That is the first step."

I took my turn to join the party of stares again and noticed that Mr. Bolden was talking. His hooded guest made no movement and gave no appearance that he was taking part in the conversation. I could hear Mr. Bolden's voice, but nothing else.

"What's the second step?"

"Oh, probably getting him to talk and act like a human. I think we are still a few days away from that." She gave a sideway glance in their direction. "Once we are past that, we will try to integrate him with you guys and see how that goes."

"Then the others?" I asked.

"We will see. That is a long way down the road." She put the magazine down flat in her lap. "So enough about that. How was your first dark magic class?"

"Interesting. I think I am a danger."

"So, the council was right?" Jennifer asked with a giggle.

"In a way. Seems my mother taught me a lot and I need to complete my training to not just know how to use it, but how to use it properly. There are a lot of rules, and not the council's either. These are rules of the universe," I said with the duck incident still firmly in my head, and that was only one of many examples I ran into where I didn't fully understand the implications of using a particular spell. "Even more interesting, they called what my mother taught me old magic, or the old ways, which I guess makes sense, but they said it really isn't taught or used anymore."

"This isn't something any of the others are learning?"

"Well, maybe Lisa, I guess, but not the others. They say they won't have the ability or power to wield it."

"Well, don't tell Gwen that. She'll have a fit," remarked Jennifer. I rolled my black eyes.

Apryl spun around. "What about Gwen?"

"Nothing. Go back to ogling whatever is happening back there," I directed and, surprisingly, she gave up on hearing what she thought was dirt on Gwen and went back to focusing on the other end of the deck.

"Anyway, it's going to take a lot of extra work after my normal classes to learn all I need to learn." I surprised myself with an exacerbated faux sigh that was completely unplanned.

"So how are things going with young Nathan?" She asked with a curious curling up of one side of her lip. It had only been a few weeks since I had stopped thinking of her as an adult or instructor and more of as a friend. I was older than her, but it still felt odd to have girl-talk with her on this topic.

"Well, he is grounded for everything except our time with Amy, but the plus is that gives me plenty of time to spend in my extra class." I faked a smile and gave two big thumbs-up. "Beyond that, it's complicated."

Jennifer took the magazine out of her lap and laid it on the table next to her and shifted toward me, leaning her chin on the arm propped up on the arm of the chair. "How so? Tell me about it. I know a little something about relationships." Her eyes popped toward her husband, who was sitting at the other end of the deck.

"Just complicated."

"They always are," she said. "That is the nature of a relationship. We have been together for forty-three years. There have been good moments and bad moments. They go hand in hand with each other. You need to remember; you are both individuals with your own quirks and personalities. Sometimes those complement each other, other times those rub against each other."

"That is the problem. We are individuals and different." I sank back into my seat.

"Being different can be good," Jennifer said, but I sat up and interrupted her to help her understand the problem.

"No, we are *different*," I said with air quotes, and then smiled to show my fangs.

"Oh?" she questioned, then her face cringed before she let out an even louder, "Oh!" She leaned over closer. "He has a problem with you being a vampire?" she asked, surprised. "He has always known you were one."

I shook my head and explained. "The problem is, he isn't." Her response was a pinched quizzical look, which told me I needed to explain further. "We are fine now, but in say thirty years..."

I let that hang there while I watched the wheels inside her mind turn. Once the gears clicked together, the light came on, and the quizzical look was gone. Her face was still pinched as she sat back and gave another, "Oh!"

"Yea. Sir, why are you kissing your daughter like that?" I said and then smirked awkwardly. "Add another twenty and I would be his granddaughter." Then I added a thought that before recently I hadn't really considered. I believed I could thank Amy for that. "And if we were ever to have kids, they would quickly grow older than me. Maybe they would, maybe they wouldn't. Hell, I don't even know if that is even possible, and if it is, what will it be?"

I threw my hands up and collapsed back in my chair, hard, causing its legs to squeak against the floor. My hands covered my face and tried to rub some clarity in to my thoughts. An act that hadn't worked at all over the last several weeks, but yet I still attempted the fruitless action. Through my hands, I asked, "Is it even possible?"

When I didn't hear a response, I peeked through my fingers at Jennifer. She looked back blankly. When I dropped my hands, she gave me a noncommittal, "I don't know. I only know of vampire and vampire couples, and they can't, but we don't understand why not. Nathan is a human, which changes a part of the equation."

"Great, if I am not a weapon of mass destruction, I am the land of a thousand mysteries," I remarked, again covering my face with my hands.

"And your other problem..." started Jennifer before a sound at the other end of the deck interrupted her, and everyone else. All heads turned in that direction and saw our new guest standing up with an aggressive stance. Mr. Bolden matched it. Mike and Brad both leaped to their feet, but Jennifer called them both off. "Mike. Brad. Let Kevin deal with it." Both boys settled down back in their seats, but their attention remained on the scene.

"Anyway, your other problem," she continued, and I turned my attention back to her. "There are things we can do to help, for a while. Make-up tricks. But that will only work for so long, and yes, eventually he will age to a point, and you will have to also deal with something else too."

I gulped at that thought. My mind hadn't made it to that point yet. It was still trying to get over how we would look when he was eighty. What happened after wasn't much of a thought yet. Now it both consumed and terrified me.

"Does Nathan know you have these concerns?"

"They're his," I said pointedly. "Well, the ones about aging are. The ones about having children are mine."

Jennifer smiled at me, and I braced myself for a joke coming at my expense. "I don't know if we have ever had a wedding in the coven before."

"Whoa, now slow up." I felt my body wanting to crawl up and out of the chair.

"What?" she feigned innocence. "It is obvious you are both thinking about a future with each other. That is just the next natural step."

"Thinking about maybe, but ready for it, I am not sure. Wouldn't we need to work through that kind of big issue first?"

"Maybe, and maybe not," she quipped. "Look, the only thing I can tell you for sure about love is don't over think it. Just go with it. As soon as you over think it, you will ruin that warm feeling it wraps you with."

And here we are again, another person telling me, the queen of over thinking, to not over think something. I didn't doubt she was right. I knew she was. When I just let things happen, I was, and felt, happier. It was me trying to solve these issues, or focusing on these issues, which stole that feeling away. I knew it would be hard to do, but I had to try. What choice did I have? There was one, but letting Nathan go was the one reality I couldn't accept. "I will try."

"Good. Don't let *you* ruin what could be the best thing to have happened to you in a while. You deserve this." She leaned over and gave me a hug. When she did, she whispered, "You really do deserve this. Enjoy it. Our lives are hard enough as it is. Don't make it any harder than it needs to be."

Whether I did or didn't deserve it, I wasn't sure, but who was I to stand in the way?

3

Another day and another schedule full of classes and then some. At first, I was a little intimidated by the extra work and the attention it brought. Failure was absolutely an option, but the more I remembered, the stronger the connection I felt with my mother and who I really was. That turned it into a longing to learn more, and to learn faster. Master Thomas was a cold wet blanket more than once. His admonishments to wait or slowdown, when I was ready to move on to learn what was next, turned out to be prudent. There were depths of the topic that I was not seeing. I guessed that was why he was called Master.

Only spending time with Nathan rivaled the exhilaration I felt learning. My little talk with Jennifer, which lasted all night, about our little difference helped me put things into perspective, and even made me feel a little silly. Maybe I was blowing it up to be more than it really was. It wouldn't be the first time, and I was sure it wouldn't be the last time. I just needed to make sure this time when I took a smoldering fire and blew it up into a full-blown forest fire, I didn't burn down everything I really cared about.

Before I made it to either, I had to make it through my normal classes and my witch's school, where I needed to heed the warning Mrs. Saxon gave me two days ago about showing off. I didn't really realize I was doing it. Well, maybe I did. Okay, I will admit it. I did. I completely did and made sure Gwen got an eyeful every time I did it.

The spells and uses of magic Mrs. Saxon taught to these teenagers were ones I learned when I was less than half their age. It had been a while since I used them, but after a quick refresher, I found most, not all, came back quickly, making any class assignments relatively easy. This meant I had opportunities. First showing how easily something came to me, which absolutely frustrated the queen-B. Then I had time while everyone else was practicing. What is it they say, idle hands are devil's playthings? Well, mine weren't the devil's, but they were my playthings. So, from time to time, I tried a few other things I knew. Like throwing voices all around her, or even my favorite, a form of glamour to make everyone in the room look exactly like Gwen. Of course, no one saw it except Gwen. To Mrs. Tenderschott, Marcia, Tera, Lisa, and Jack, nothing had changed, but everywhere Gwen looked she saw her reflection, right down to the attitude. She didn't seem to enjoy having the Gwen we saw reflected back at her. I broke down later that day and told Jack what I did. I am not sure who had more enjoyment out of it, him, or me. I knew what she was reacting to, and he could feel the frustration building inside her.

Even though I never admitted what I did to anyone else, and I knew Jack wouldn't rat me out – we had grown a little closer which seemed to rub Nathan and his damn jealousy the wrong way at times, I was fairly sure Gwen knew it was me. Not that it could have really been anyone else. Most were still struggling with some of the basics. Only Lisa seemed to progress relatively quickly, and my little pranks appeared to annoy her.

How Gwen reacted to me in Mr. Helms' classes after each of my little private torture sessions dismissed any illusion I had about Gwen not knowing I was behind it all. She was a little extra amped up when we sparred, which Mr. Helms seemed to encourage when he noticed, and she caught me off guard more than a few times. Even with my enhanced speed, she got close, and I swore once I smelled the distinctive odor of singed hair. I gave it back as good as she gave, and I will admit I let things get a little out of control when I had finally had it and unloaded a new trick and turned Gwen's stomach. That girl vomited everywhere, stopping everyone else, and drawing the ire of Mr. Helms. We weren't really supposed to hurt anyone. I wasn't sure he bought my counter argument that I didn't really hurt her. Needless to say, it was going to be a few days before I ventured down to the witch's floor to hang out.

My plan for the day was to be on my best behavior. Though the best laid plans were meant to be broken. Just like my plan to have a lovely day went down the toilet as soon as I touched the door handle on my way out to the hall. Why this was happening now? I didn't know. It blew the growing theory I had about why it had happened in the past right out of the door. I wasn't upset or vulnerable at all, at least I wasn't until the door handle turned into the hand of Jean St. Claire and the room around me became some kind of dark gothic cathedral complete with dank moist mildew filled air. A stark contrast to the white palatial estate I last found myself in when he butted into my life. That was one of his more pleasant visits, and he even brought guests who appeared dressed for a party and stood around as he explained that I had him all wrong. That life with him was a promise of a grand future. I wouldn't mind hearing that one again instead of having him creeping forward through what was my door, and me having to yank free from his cold grip. I scurried back as far as I could, to where my bed should have been, but found an algae laced stone wall.

"Larissa, it is inevitable. Today, tomorrow, centuries from now. Whether you join me on your own, or I finally strip you of what I desire. It will eventually happen. I have all the time in the world."

His voice echoed while a host of other dark eyed vampires gathered behind him. They circled around him and then spread out, surrounding me. Each reached for me.

The chorus of the soulless called my name in a symphony of hell. There was something demonically melodic about how the air around me vibrated with each syllable. My fingers scratched at the floor to escape their procession toward me, but before I knew it, they were behind me, beside me, and in front of me, with Jean St. Claire leading the way. The sound of my name from their voices took on a rhythmic sound, almost like a drumbeat. Not a heartbeat, with that little irregular thump-thump followed by a long pause and then two more. This was thump, pause, thump, pause. As if my own name was being pounded into me. Then it all faded away, leaving my room and the pounding. That was when I screamed.

None of the prior visits from Jean St. Claire had caused me to scream. This one had though. Coming out of that little scene more than a bit spooked and seeing two sets of rage filled black eyes staring at me from beyond the door in my closet sent me over the edge. The thumping, his fist pounding on the magical barrier that kept someone like him, male, from coming through.

That scream brought Apryl, Laura, and Jennifer bursting through my door. The sight of this individual and the sound of his assault brought them all to a standstill. His blonde hair hung down over his face. Two dark eyes seethed underneath his straggly locks. The two lips that made up his mouth snarled. Behind him, two hands grabbed him and pulled him back up the stairs. His eyes remained locked on me, never moving. Even through the quick struggle, they stayed fixed right on me. Once he gave in to Mr. Bolden's grasp, he disappeared.

"Sorry, he got away while I was in the shower," yelled Mr. Bolden. His voice told of the strain it took to restrain our new guest.

"Not yet ready to mingle, I see," I remarked, and took Jennifer's hand as she helped me back up to my feet.

"Not even close," she remarked. She hung on to my hand longer than she needed to and regarded me in a peculiar way. "You're shaking."

I yanked my hand back. "He startled me. That's all." I left out the details of my other visitor.

"The big bad Larissa scared of a little vampire," Apryl laughed, but I quickly quieted that with a light shove out the door. She took it good-naturedly and was standing outside tapping her foot when I opened it to head down to class.

At the bottom of the stairs, Jennifer bid her adieu for the morning. "I will see you girls later. I think Kevin is going to need my help today."

We started for the hallway and out of the magical snowfall until I had to stop and do a double take. A small fir tree had sprouted in the middle of the marble floor of the grand entrance. I made my way over to the tree while Apryl and Laura watched. After a quick walk around it, admiring its snow kissed branches, I pointed at it and said, "Don't tell me." They didn't have to. I knew what it was.

Classes went on with no other disturbances, and I felt just minorly distracted. Nathan only asked me what was wrong twice and dismissed it as being because of my little closet visitor. I knew how Nathan got when I brought up issues or questions from my past, and after answering the questions related to Mrs. Norton on our little trip, I was fairly sure he believed that was the last of that drama. You would think he would know his girlfriend better. Of course, I was an expert at hiding stuff, and with him, all it took was a simple holding of hands or kiss to settle things down. Not that he was simple. He wasn't, and neither was our relationship. It wasn't one of those puppy love things built on such shallow acts. He got me, and I got him. That was it. Our personalities clicked from day one, and they still did. Neither of us had any fears of opening up with the other and talking about our deepest concerns and fears. Hell, that first night we dove right into the deep end and never came up for a breath. I think the little things, like holding hands, calmed his concerns because he knew physical touch was something that took trust between us, and each time I did, it was an unwritten way for me to ask him to trust me. In some strange and twisted version of the definition, touch was our love language.

While the others broke for lunch before our afternoon of *Witch 101*, I had another errand to run. I sat there with Nathan for a bit as he ate, but then flatly told him the truth, or a form of the truth. I had something I wanted to talk to Mr. Demius about before class. Nathan didn't bat an eye at hearing this, and of course I kissed him bye.

It was the truth. I had something I wanted to talk to him about. It was something that came to me during the middle of history class. Possibly a solution to one of my many issues. At best, a respite, which to me would be like a vacation in heaven.

I entered his class and called his name, but there was no answer. I walked toward the front of the classroom and called for him yet again. I found it odd that he wasn't there. Mr. Demius was not someone you ran into around the coven, and he appeared to keep mostly to himself. Just to make sure, I let my other side listen, and there it was. The beat and the sound of fluid running through very narrow veins. It called to me, and even tickled the back of my throat. Good thing we had another hunting session in a few days. Neither of his life-giving actions were rushed. They were slow and relaxed, and it made me wonder if he was asleep. Which was a possibility. To my knowledge, he didn't have classes at this time of day. I started to leave, not wanting to wake him, but then I heard his voice mumble something from one of the alcoves to the right.

What I approached was a sight I wasn't expecting. There in the darkness was a room with a storm raging overhead. Clouds swirled and lightning flashed in the small room illuminating the scene below it in momentary snapshots of some occult ceremony. Below it, Mr. Demius knelt around a crystal ball with seven other translucent figures. Each knelt like he was. Each dressed like he was, too. I tried to cling to the wall to avoid being seen, but failed. One of the other individuals looked up just as I peeked around the corner. Our eyes locked. Mine black and emotionless, his empty. I ducked back around the corner and clung to the wall, hoping that he missed me, but knowing he didn't.

It wasn't long before I heard two very precise footsteps coming in my direction. When I heard my name, I wanted to shrink down and disappear through one of the cracks in the floor. I am sure that was something that was possible, but it wasn't a skill I had acquired yet.

"Miss Dubois, is that you?"

I finally stepped out from behind the wall and out into the archway. "Sorry, Mr. Demius, I didn't mean to interrupt." I hurriedly apologized, fully expecting to take his fury, and rightfully so. My intrusion was just that. This was his classroom, his chamber, and when he didn't respond to my calling his name, I should have left, and not snooped around, no matter what I felt. Not to mention what I had walked in on.

Behind him the translucent members of his circle disappeared, and the storm, ball, and the rest of the scene faded, leaving just a plain empty room with stone floor and walls. "Not a problem. What can I do for you?"

My gaze was still focused on the scene, or where the scene had been, over his shoulder. "I am really sorry; I just had a question I was wondering if you could help..." I started but found it hard to focus on the question I needed to ask, and to ignore what I had seen. "I'm sorry, but were those spirits?" I blurted out, unable to control the diarrhea of my thoughts.

"Some were. Some were my associates," Mr. Demius said. "It is important to be in contact with those of our past, present, and future. What you saw was just that. A gathering of sorts." He walked into the main area of his classroom and paused at the altar-like table that was at the front. "Some were my counterparts around the world, and some were from my past. It is important to embrace both Miss Dubois. I would like for you to understand that."

"Yes sir," I said, still shaken by the empty eyes that stared back at me.

"Now, what brought you here so early? I doubt you are eager for this much extra work."

I took a moment, which was probably longer to me than him, to pull myself together before asking the real reason I was here. "I was hoping you would be able to show me how to use the solar cross."

I had no idea there was a more serious look on Mr. Demius' face than his normal expression. This expression bordered on a scowl as he regarded me and my request. "For what?" he questioned curiously.

"Protection."

"From St. Claire?" he inquired with the same curious tone.

"Yes. From both his physical and other visits."

It was that answer that released the curious scowl from his expression. "I see. Is he still reaching out?"

I hadn't mentioned it, nor had anyone asked, over the last couple of days. Nothing had really changed, and nothing about his messages made me believe the threat was any stronger now than it had ever been, so it wasn't something I really felt needed to be reported, and in the past reporting it always led to a ton of queries, but I needed to own up to it now. "Yes, not as often as before..." I started, but Mr. Demius completed my thought.

"But now that you remember the solar cross, you would like to use it to close the door all together."

"Yes, sir. Would it work?" I inquired hopefully.

"If applied right, it can't be broken, in most cases."

"In most cases?"

"Yes, everything in this world is all about power and the focus of that power."

There was that word again, but luckily for me, I felt I had a better handle on my focus now.

"It will all depend on how strong and focused you are when you apply it. I don't doubt you could block him out, but there is another part of this equation we have to consider. How strong and focused the other side of it is. Remember, Mrs. Tenderschott believed he was using voodoo, true dark magic, to make his entrance. I believe this is correct in that assumption. How effective your protection will be depends on how strong the person helping him is," he explained. "But that is not to say we shouldn't try. Shall we?"

4

I was more than a few minutes late coming down for our nightly story time with Amy. It hadn't been that long since I last took off, so I was surprised they hadn't sent a search party out looking for me, or come looking themselves. I had promised both Amy and Nathan I wouldn't run away again, and I meant it, but I had a feeling things were still a little raw from the last time giving me a lot to make up for with those two, and it was more than just earning their trust again.

Putting the runes in place took most of my afternoon and some of the evening. There was a lot more to it than just writing them on my door. Wait, I needed to correct that. You don't write a rune, at least not one that will work. You place it. The placing of a rune involved a specific sequence of events and movements. Before you ever picked up the pen, you had to clear the room of all negative energy, spirits, and presences. As Mr. Demius said, you don't want to trap them inside when you are done. That made perfect sense to me. To do that, you smudged the room with a combination of herbs that he sent me to Mrs. Tenderschott for. I found my heightened sense of smell was a curse during this activity. The smell was not pungent, but it was... how can I say it? Harsh? Invading? Penetrating? All the above. It would have been strong enough to sting the nostrils of a normal human. It burned mine to the point of tears.

Once that was done, and the accompanying prayer said, which was what Mr. Demius called it, but it sounded like a spell to me, only then were you able to place the actual rune, and even that had its complications. Every symbol had to be drawn in a certain way. Take the solar cross as an example. It is a circle with a cross running in the center, its arms extending out of the circle. If you drew the circle first, it wouldn't work. If you drew the cross and then the circle, it wouldn't work either. The motion had to be a single fluid motion, start at the bottom of the cross, up, back to the center, out to the left, back to the center, then out to the right, and then back to the center. All without lifting the pen. Then you retraced back out to the left until you were midway down that arm and drew an arc intersecting each arm of the cross, and as you did, you drew back into the center and out again before you continued. Mr. Demius said to think of the symbol as a building. Its layers gave it strength. The single motion meant it was a continuous structure with only one beginning and end, which closed off all entries and exits. The particular rune he had me use was only two symbols, the solar cross and the besom, which was a lot less complicated than the solar cross. It only involved one movement.

After I placed the symbols, there was another smudging, with another set of herbs that were no less fragrant, and no less painful to do. Then there was the spell. Which, as he said, was where the real magic happened. I stood in the center of my room, held the images of both symbols in my hand, and repeated, "I create a place that is safe for me to live. Free from dark spirits and intruders. Those that attempt to cross will pay a dear price." When I completed the words, the runes burned, and became one with the door I had placed them on, fading into the wood. This was the old way, which he felt was appropriate for me to use.

By the time I was done, it was dark outside my window. I looked up at the clock and realized there were only twelve minutes until Amy's bedtime. I couldn't miss the opportunity to see her. Even those few minutes would be precious. I rushed down the stairs, past the tree that had grown another four feet since the afternoon, and through the strong snowstorm that covered our entry. The snow didn't stop when I opened the door and headed out. The coolness of fall had given way to the first snowfall of the season. A magical carpet of white covered everything except the pool deck and the pool. I saw Nathan and Amy sitting at the table, her in his lap being read to like always. The opportunity was too golden to miss.

Two lightly packed snowballs crashed into the back of Nathan, prompting a slight jump from him. They were both light tosses. I didn't want to send him flying across the deck with Amy in his arms. She looked back over his shoulder and started laughing as she saw another in my hand about to fly. The surprise was gone, but that took nothing from it, and I let it fly, hitting Nathan right in the back. I heard their laughter as I walked up behind them.

"Hey Larissa," cried Amy.

I leaned over Nathan to give her a hug and him a quick kiss. She hung on to me as I pulled back up and I lifted her away from Nathan's lap. He stood up and let what snow remained on his back fall away. His body jerked each time a wet spot on his shirt hit him. I felt a little bad, but still couldn't stop myself from laughing. Neither could Amy. I looked across at Amy's escort, and she seemed to approve of my holding her. Well, maybe not approve. She just didn't object outwardly.

"So, what are you guys reading?" I asked as I sat down with Amy across the table from Nathan, and closer to the fire he had going in the pit. I wouldn't feel the cold, but Amy would, and I wasn't providing her any warmth.

She proudly held up the book. It was something new that I hadn't seen her with before.

"I thought we could use something different, and Edward suggested these," replied Nathan. That meant two people were using the library.

Amy handed the book to me, and I quickly recognized the cover. "Oh, I loved Nancy Drew." I did. Mrs. Norton had the complete collection. She said she bought it from a used bookstore in town just for me. I must have read each of them a dozen times or more. "The Secret of the Old Clock. I can't tell you how many times I read this. I loved it."

She opened it up to where she and Nathan had been before my little interruption. I picked up right there and started reading. Feeling her nuzzle against me while I read those words, words I had read sitting in my room, down in our library, and out in the woods back at my home, was more than a little fulfilling. All seemed right with the world. The glow I felt took away some of the sting of seeing her being led away by Ms. Parrish once we were done. It also distracted me, so I didn't smell what was coming up behind me, and didn't expect to be the target myself of a large snowball, right in the back of my head.

I spun around in a way that sent the chair skittering across the concrete pool deck. Rob stood there with another one in hand, looking rather proud of himself. That was only momentary. Before he could launch, two were on their way at him, and knowing he could take it, I didn't hold back. The first one hit him and forced him to stumble backward. The second put him on his butt. Now it was my turn to feel rather proud of myself. I never saw the Martins coming at me. The game was on.

The four of us exchanged volleys back and forth, me having to make sure I remembered who I was throwing at to avoid hurting Nathan. To make it fair, I didn't use any magic to block or help, and took my fair share of frozen projectiles, all while laughing the whole time. This was my first snowball fight, ever! It never snowed in New Orleans, and the only times it did in Virginia, it was this messy sleet stuff that you couldn't really make a snowball out of without including a ton of ice and dirt. That explained why the snowman I made once was gray and not white.

It was a pretty even fight until balls started raining down on us from above. I looked up and saw two sources of the new aerial attack. Jack, Tera, and Gwen were on one side of their outdoor balcony, and Lisa and Marcia were on the other. All five were ignoring my self-imposed no magic rule. They were gathering the falling snow into balls and sending them our way. Nathan and I quickly took shelter under the umbrella over the table we sat at with Amy. Martin and Robert did the same at another. Snowballs continued to thud on the canvas tops. Off in the distance, Mr. Markinson and Dan emerged from the woods and phased into their more recognizable states. Dan stood there for a few moments before Mr. Markinson encouraged him to go on. He laughed as he watched Dan head to provide back-up to the others. Before he reached the table, he lobbed a few snowballs all the way up to the balcony coming relatively close to queen Gwen. That was probably why a storm of snowballs blew up over them, giving Nathan and me an opportunity to run for the door. Of course, I didn't expect an attack from the top deck coming down on us. We made it to the door, only suffering a few hits. Our clothes were soaked thanks to the melted snow, and I knew Nathan had to be freezing now. I pulled him in close, even though I knew I wouldn't be able to stop his shivering. I wish I could have.

For his health, we called it a night, and I walked him to his door, and told him good night there, with a kiss and a snide remark. "You better go in before your chaperone comes to get you."

He gave me the same little wry smile he had for the duration of his sentence. When the door closed, I took off running down the hall and up the stairs. I still needed to get a few more shots in. I changed into some dry clothes as I flashed through my room, and quickly joined the others on the deck who were still all at the railing. Not a one saw me, at least not until the snowballs hit them from behind, then they knew I was there and turned around with their hands up surrendering. That may have had something to do with the few dozens of snowballs that were hovering behind me just waiting. I didn't take any prisoners, but easily welcomed each of my laughing friends to my side and joined them at the railing to continue to pummel Rob, Martin, and Dan until they got inside. Mr. Markinson crossed the pool deck with a cautious look up. The snowball barrage from below us had stopped. My newfound alliance members each stopped and looked at me, expecting me to take a shot at him. I guess that was expected since I had put him through a wall once.

The rest of the night we made snow vampires, of course. Snowmen with fangs in various humorous and bordering on obnoxious positions and poses. All Jennifer could do was roll her eyes at some of the sophomoric humor going on, but it got everyone laughing, and that felt good.

Laura and I were making snow angels in an undisturbed area of the deck when I felt a presence standing over me. I opened my eyes and stared up at two dark eyes looking down at me from behind stringy blonde hair shoved in the hood of a black hoodie. I jumped up, as did Laura, and we both took a quick step back.

Mr. Bolden stood next to him, seemingly ready to pounce if needed. "Larissa, Clay has something he would like to say."

Clay appeared to be an individual bordering on hostilities, much like I had seen at the door to my closet this morning. Every muscle in his body appeared to twitch. Even his fingers flexed in what I could only imagine was an attempt at finding some kind of control.

"Go on," encouraged Mr. Bolden.

He said nothing. His black eyes jumped back and forth between Laura and me. I was certain there was hostile intent behind them.

"Clay?" Mr. Bolden prompted, and then gave him a little shove with his elbow.

I half expected our newest member to put Mr. Bolden on the ground, but instead, all the angst we had seen in him appeared to melt away. He closed his eyes, and when they opened again, all the twitching of his muscles was gone, and we were looking at a different person. "I am sorry if I scared you earlier," apologized the surprisingly calm and syrupy southern voice. His drawl was so deep that I doubted anything he said could sound mean or angry coming out.

"It's okay," I said. "I'm Larissa." I held out my hand to him, and his eyes watched it nervously and conflicted.

My hand hung there in an awkward silence that neither of us appeared to know how to break. Over his shoulder, I saw someone else watching nervously. Mr. Bolden rescued us. "Clay, Larissa, is new around here too, and you two have something else in common."

Seeing the open door Mr. Bolden just presented, I walked right through. "We do?"

It was immediately obvious Clay wasn't coming through the door with me. His expression hadn't changed. He was still fixated on my hand, so I withdrew it, hoping that would free him, but it didn't. Instead, his eyes now looked at my own with the same nervous and conflicted stare.

"Yes, he is from the south too," Mr. Bolden finally said, giving up on Clay to be an active participant in this conversation. "He is from Gulfport, Mississippi. Clay, Larissa is from New Orleans." It didn't seem important to clarify that was over a century ago, and I spent most of my life in Virginia.

I waited a few more moments to see if Clay would say anything, but his mouth appeared clamped shut. Nothing I said would pull him out, and I looked up at Mr. Bolden for direction. He mouthed back, 'say goodbye.'

Instead of just saying goodbye, I took a more polite and cordial route. "That is so cool. Well, it is nice to meet you."

Mr. Bolden reached up and grabbed Clay by the shoulder. I prepared to help, expecting some kind of physical altercation, but he quietly turned around, shuffling his feet like some kind of zombie that let Mr. Bolden lead him down toward the other end of the deck where they held camp each night. Then he pulled free and jumped back in our direction. I felt my knees flex. Laura stepped back another few steps, giving him some room. Mr. Bolden rushed back to intercept Clay, but he was too late. By the time Mr. Bolden arrived, Clay had already made his big move, and reached forward, grabbing my hand.

"It's nice to meet you too," he stuttered. Then just as suddenly he released it and headed back to the other end of the deck, with Mr. Bolden in tow.

"What was that about?" Laura asked.

"Let's say, no progress on step two yet."

5

The saying is, "necessity is the mother of invention," but with Tera and Marcia, necessity was the mother of forgiveness. All of my little pranks on Gwen were forgotten as soon as the entire witch squad struggled with Mrs. Saxon's latest assignment. Seeing me perform it flawlessly earned me a few evil looks before it earned me an invitation to the witch's floor after my extra schoolwork. The invite didn't come from Gwen. No surprise there. She wasn't even there when Marcia and Tera asked, but neither hid the fact that all of them wanted me to stop by. My biggest challenge was not showing them; it was not enjoying it too much.

To be honest, I wasn't really sure why Mrs. Saxon taught this particular skill. It could be even seen as irresponsible, not that it didn't have its uses. I was sure it did. She just didn't come out and say what those were, at least not clearly, and left us to wonder about it, and that made me uncomfortable. Not about me, but about the others.

There was no one in the hall when I stepped through the door of the witch's floor for the first time since our last telepathy contest, but I heard the murmur coming from the door to the common room. It all went silent as soon as I stepped in. A far too common reaction to my walking in a room for my liking. There were five silent witches sitting on the various sofas watching as I walked to the center of the room, and there it was again, another awkward silence. I hated those and wondered if I was the source of all the ones I encountered. To rescue myself from this one, I asked, "So, you guys wanted me to help you with compulsion?"

"Yes, please," responded Jack. His response was sugary sweet and topped with an over-baked smile. He was one I was rather shocked to see have a problem with it. Something about his empath ability made him the perfect candidate for this, or so I thought. Plus, there was a joke Apryl once made about watching out for him planting thoughts in our heads.

"All right," I said while I let my shoulders slump, hoping to let the stress I felt from my standoffish reception drip down my arms and out of me. "What part of it are you struggling with?" I directed my question at Jack who I hoped was still somewhat in what I would call my circle of friends.

"Everything," he exclaimed desperately and then leaned forward in his seat. "I tried all afternoon to put suggestions in everyone's mind, and not a one felt anything."

Sometimes the best way to teach someone how to do something is to show them. I whispered my suggestion to only myself and watched Jack stand up, to his own amazement. "What did you feel?" I asked him.

"You. I heard your voice, just before my body leaned forward and stood up." He stood there, lifting each leg as if to check to make sure he had control of them again.

"That is because I whispered it into your mind. That is the key," I explained, strangely feeling more like a teacher than a peer as I walked a few steps toward the others. "When my mother taught me this, she made me practice just talking to her that way for a long time before she let me plant a suggestion. And trust me, it was a case of her letting me. I tried a few times to have her hand me something, or do something humorous like moo like a cow, but she caught me each time." I said, hoping to loosen the crowd up. Jokes were supposed to do that, but it didn't work here.

"Why don't we practice just doing that? It's not exactly the same as the witch whisper, but similar enough. Instead of trying to think about sending it through a wall or to some place, think about the person." I looked around the room. "Marcia, why don't you and Lisa try it? Tera and Gwen. Jack, since I have already done it to you, let's pair up."

The next several minutes sounded like an old television commercial for a phone company. "Could you hear me?" The response was always "No." The level of exasperation increased each time. I remembered it took me a while at first and I passed more than a few levels of frustration. Several piles of dirt and patches of weeds out in our field paid the price.

I tried to remember if my mother had given me any pointers on this part. She didn't. It was just hours and days of practice. Probably not what this room full of frustrated witches wanted to hear. Not that Mrs. Saxon didn't warn them. I couldn't remember exactly how long it took me. That was when it hit me, and I exclaimed, "That is it!"

"You heard me?" Jack asked excitedly. He was about to jump out of his skin, and I felt bad that I was going to have to delay his celebration a little.

"No," I said and watched him shrink. He looked like a little boy that just watched someone run over his puppy. The rest of the room stood silent and stunned. "I know why Mrs. Saxon taught us this."

My revelation prompted several confused looks. "This is a very dangerous skill to know. The ability to plant a thought and make someone do something against their will. It is something that could be abused," I said and instantly felt concerned for even saying that out loud, and hoped I hadn't planted any thoughts in their minds. To try to recover and keep anyone else from thinking deeper about it, I completed my lecture on the topic. "My mother told me it was only to be used if we felt someone was about to realize who we really were, and that was it. I was never to use it for any other purpose other than to keep people from finding out what we really are."

I was proud for a moment. I remembered the why behind one of mother's lessons. The others could have cared less and resumed their practice mildly more annoyed than before. None were being successful. From what I could tell, not a one of them was even close. I took a break from being Jack's partner to walk around and observe the others, which was a good thing. I caught Marcia doing something that I had when I was learning. "Don't say it out loud. They need to hear it with their mind, and not their ears."

I went back to being Jack's dummy, never once hearing his suggestion in my head. He had now resorted to leaning toward me, as if closing the distance between us would help. I hated to break it to him. Distance didn't matter, but even after he backed up, it wasn't more than a few seconds before he leaned forward again. I was about to correct him again when I saw something out of the corner of my eye. Gwen sat down. Now did she sit down on her own, or did Tera do it? I looked over at them curiously and knew my answer when Tera turned around, smiling.

"Gwen, are you okay?" I asked. The entire room was now staring in her direction.

"Yes, why?"

"You sat down."

She jumped up from the sofa and spun around and looked at it before she turned and looked at Tera. All she did was point at her, and Tera nodded. That was the flicker in the room that set the rest on fire. All asking Tera how she did it. Which was something I had to hear too. How to explain something like this was like explaining how air tasted or breathing happened. It just happened, but once it did, then you knew the clue, and that was all it took to be able to do it over and over again.

"I don't know. It just happened," she explained, just like every other witch who had ever tried to explain it through the history of time.

The good news was, there was now another witch that could do it and could be the focus of their questions, letting me off the hook, kind of. Each time I tried to slip out, someone would ask if they could try it on me one more time, which meant they stood there staring at me hopefully, to start, and disappointed to finish. It was when I finally made my escape that Jack yelled, "it worked."

That prompted me to stand there in the door just a few seconds longer to see if he truly got it.

"I told you to leave, and you did," he said with a big grin.

"Ha!" I left through the hall and down the stairs to meet Nathan for our few moments with Amy. Something about reading her one of my childhood favorites last night had me thinking about those stories all day, and I couldn't wait to sit there and read her some more. My mind was already deep into thinking about the story when Edward's voice called my name in the grand entry. "Larissa."

I turned and saw his head hovering over the tree that was now a good fifteen feet tall. The sight of his head as a tree topper made me giggle. Edward looked around for the source of my amusement and when he spotted his location, he shifted to the right, "Hmmm." He didn't appear to share my amusement. "Larissa, I found some information in response to your query about the Nortons."

I quickly shushed him and held up a hand to keep him quiet while I looked outside to make sure Nathan was already out there, and well out of ear shot of anything we might say. That was one battle I didn't want to relive. "Sorry about that. What did you find?"

"Nothing in the archives, but I stumbled across their names, and cross referenced a few sources to validate it was them. It was in human documentation. Birth certificates, wedding licenses, and newspapers. Thomas Norton was born on March 23, 1845. He grew up to be a prominent carpenter, building cabinets and fine furnishing. Marie Abbot was born on December 17, 1847, and became a schoolteacher in 1867, part of a new class of teachers that was reported on in the paper. They wedded on May 19, 1869, right there in New Orleans. The only other reference to them was a report on their disappearance three days after their wedding, as part of an article about a series of disappearances in the area. It's not much, but that is all I could find. I am sorry. There isn't anything else. Would you like to look over those references? I can have them sent to your room."

"Yes, please," I said enthusiastically. I knew these weren't earth shattering details, but it was something, and that was better than what I had. "Go ahead and put it on top of the other books in my room."

"Yes ma'am... and I understand you have a note that Mrs. Norton wrote with her own hand. Is that correct?"

"Yes. I do."

"Then there is something on page 281 of the second book you might find interesting." With that, Edward disappeared, leaving me to wonder what was on that page, while the tree grew another foot.

I was a little distracted the rest of the night, not to say I didn't enjoy things. I did. How could I not? Those thirty minutes we spent together were the best moments of my day. It was why I got up... I mean, why I got dressed in the morning. The more we did it, the more my mind wandered and thought of us as a family. Maybe it was the glow of the moment outshining the truth, but even Ms. Parrish seemed to warm up as she brought Amy down and took her back up. That might be stretching it. She just wasn't as frigid as normal, and the leers and sneers were now few and far between.

Just as always, Nathan and I lingered a little outside and then walked in slowly. This would be our time, and the only time we were really alone while he was under house arrest. Though Nathan hinted that his mother had mentioned loosening up the conditions a bit, but hadn't provided any definitive timelines for his parole.

The lingering normally lasted a little in the entry way too, until we parted, but my little distraction pulled at me to head up the stairs, and I desperately wanted to cut it short.

"Okay bye." I gave him a quick kiss and attempted to head for the stairs.

Nathan had other ideas and grabbed my hand and pulled me back against him. "Where are you going so fast?"

"I need to look up something," I said, keeping it vague. He gave me his little puppy dog eyes that he did at times when he felt I was holding something back from him. Which was better than the intense stare I received when he knew I was. So, I played into it and grabbed both of his hands, tilted my head, and said, "It's a witch thing." That was the magic trick, and I didn't even use compulsion here, not that I would have.

"The thing you went to talk to Mr. Demius about at lunch yesterday?" he asked. I nodded while I wrapped my arms around him and kissed him again. That did it, and he seemed to believe it and picked me up off the ground and spun me around while we kissed. Then he walked away, and I watched, like always, but this time feeling a little guilty. I had done it again. I had lied to Nathan, again.

6

To say I was eager to get to page 281 of that book would be the understatement of understatements. Before I even opened my door, I had already unstacked the books and opened up the second book, a large blue leather-bound book, and laid it out on my bed. Unfortunately for my impatient self, I didn't have enough control of that act to see the page numbers and open it directly to that right page. I was only three hundred pages off.

Quickly I flipped back, not paying attention to the words or the chapter titles as I did. I didn't really care what they said. I was focused on just finding that page, but I couldn't help from seeing the words relationship, family, and loved ones repeated across the pages.

When I reached the page, it was the start of a chapter called Connections. An interesting title, but not that insightful. Of course, I would need to read more to find out what was so special about this particular page, and why Edward had mentioned it. If I had learned anything about the texts that I had consulted in the library, they were never straight forward like a cookbook. It would be nice though, to have something that simply said, to do this, use this spell, with a nice little table of contents and an index to avoid making us search and hunt all around. But then again, there was something that I had heard from three very smart witches. You need to understand the why and how before you can perform the what. Like in Mrs. Tenderschott's class, she wanted us to understand the ingredients and what they meant to a potion more than the potion itself. My mother and Mrs. Saxon said the same for spells, and reading the first few paragraphs of this chapter was more of the same. All about the connections you share with people that were beyond the physical. There was the spiritual, emotional, and metaphysical. Each of those are roads or paths we can travel to connect with those we know on some level.

These words rang true with what Edward had explained was contained when he plopped them in front of me. Finding that connection was the first half of what my original request was. I wanted to use it to travel to see and talk to them, to which Edward delivered both a stiff and frightening warning. His recommendation that I look at this page led me to believe this wasn't as dangerous. Or possibly he felt I was ready for it. A simple smile crossed my face.

Another two paragraphs in, just at the bottom of the page, I saw exactly why he recommended that page, and reading the words -simplest method to—on the page removed a little of the pride, and the accompanying smile with it. Hope replaced both, though. This paragraph said if you had an object that a person touched, like an article of clothing, you could do certain checks using those connections. I kept reading, feeling more like a bloodhound than a witch. If the next sentence told me I needed to sniff it, I was going to slam the book shut, but it didn't. It went on to talk about how important it was that the object was one they touched or wore. I continued reading, and then there it was. The "Heartbeat Call" was what the spell was called. Kind of corny sounding, but reading further, I understood the name.

With the object they touched in one hand, and your other hand palm up, you read the spell while thinking of the last time you saw that person. If they were still alive, you would feel their heartbeat on the surface of your open palm.

The disappointment consumed me, and I sprung up off the bed and exclaimed, "Edward!" I didn't really intend to call him, just to voice a complaint out loud. He had forgotten a rather significant detail, and sent me on an emotional rollercoaster that ended in a heartbroken disappointment.

"Yes, Larissa. What is it?" He looked concerned from under his bushy, white eyebrows.

"I can't use this. Our heart doesn't beat anymore, remember?"

"Yes ma'am. I remember that clearly. You need to not take things so literally. This is a magical spell that will tell you if someone is still in the world of the physical. The heartbeat is a symbolic answer, not an actual heartbeat."

I stood there with my jaw falling to the floor. Was there anyone in this place who didn't have a lesson to teach me? I didn't even try to cover or act like I knew that all along. I just let it go, and walked over to my dresser, where the note had lain since I had returned. "Want to hang around for this, smarty pants?"

He gave me a humorous smile.

With the note in my right hand and my left hand held open, palm up, I thought of the last moment I saw her, the last moments on the train before I fell asleep, not the best of memories, and I repeated the spell. "Memories of the one, travel the cosmic path, and provide me a sign of your presence." The room filled with a kind of static energy, tingling all over me, and then there it was. A single thump was in my hand. Not only did I feel it, but I also heard it. A thud-thump.

I looked up at Edward, surprised that I had felt anything on so many levels. There was some doubt about what Edward had said. I seriously doubted he knew of anyone who had ever tried this to search for a vampire before. Something that seemed highly unlikely to me. But then there was the detail that sent me back on the emotional rollercoaster that I thought I had gotten off of. She was alive. Marie Norton was still alive, but where was she, and was she all right? "Does that mean...?" I started to ask, just to confirm before I climbed up any higher on the first hill of that rollercoaster. The higher I was, farther the fall.

"Yes, Larissa. It means she is alive," he replied, and I stayed in the coaster car, climbing as I jumped back on the bed, reading more to see what else I could do.

Edward hung out while I read more that tried to explain how the connection between people worked on each of the three levels of existence. It took another page until I found a list of the various types of spells I could use. With each one, the coaster car stuttered up the climb. A variation of "The Heartbeat Call" would illuminate a path on the ground to her, but she had to be within a few hundred feet. She wasn't. I could feel that much. Another would let me speak to her, which was more like an answering machine than an actual phone call. I could leave a message in a place for her, and if she ever crossed that location, she would hear it. That would work if I knew where she was. Then there was the window into a soul. I could see through their eyes, but that only worked with direct family members, which Marie Norton was not. Again, the stronger the connection, the more you can do with it. I flipped past the detailed explanations of each of those spells and found the end of the chapter. The next chapter was titled Connections of the Flesh, which I didn't feel applied here.

"Is that it?" I rolled over and asked.

"I am afraid so. That is all you can do with a note. If there was direct blood relation, we could do more. Remember, the stronger the connection..."

"... the more you can do," I completed and then fell back on my bed, trying to talk myself out of disappointment. This was good. I knew for absolutely sure she was alive and had to assume well. I just didn't know where, and that ate at me more now than ever. I shook it off and thanked Edward, who seemed to enjoy having taught me something, and then headed upstairs to join the others.

The snow vampires were still there. They now wore black capes around their backs, and someone had found black rocks to use for the eyes. That gave them a rather evil look with their overly large fangs we created out of the snow. They weren't quite demonic looking walruses, but they weren't far from it. That made even the few we did in an obscene pose more humorous. A quick glance around found everyone on the normal end of the deck, and no one on the other. Mr. Bolden and his new student hadn't come up yet, and that was okay with me. The only two encounters I had had with him so far were less than pleasant.

It was movie night, science fiction, eh, not really my first, second, or even last choice. It was a genre I never could really get into, no matter how many times Mr. Norton tried to get me into it. Mostly only the guys were paying attention to it, and by paying attention I mean they were predicting what was about to happen with constant, "watch this" or "wait for it" followed by a group cheer led by Mike. Laura, Apryl, and Pam were doing their girl talking, which at the moment I didn't feel like getting involved with. Maybe because every time I tried, the topic of Nathan came up at some point during the night. It always happened, no matter how much I tried to steer away from it. That was a topic I didn't really want to dish on, and Laura didn't really want to hear about. At times, I picked up a little jealousy from her. Not the type that was driven by a desire to be with Nathan, which oozed from every pore in Gwen's body, but from a jealousy of what I had found. On the outside, she appeared to like Mike very much, but what I sensed in her comments and even some of her unconscious reactions was she needed more.

Thanks to one of the many conversations we all had, I found out that Laura was a little bit older than the others. Pam and Apryl were relatively newborns. Each turned in just the last five years or so. Which made them really only twenty or younger. It was the same with most of the guys. They were all relatively new. Laura, she was turned back in the early nineties, almost twenty years ago, putting her really in her mid-thirties. She was ready to settle down, to have what Mr. and Mrs. Bolden have, to have what Nathan and I seemed to have. Something that I had a hard time thinking about without including Amy. A family. I knew the feeling well, and had fought against furiously. I may be ready, but it took two to tango and Nathan was still a child for all intents and purposes.

To avoid the girl talk, I followed Jennifer's lead and sat down beside where she was reading her magazine and grabbed a book. Well, not grabbed. I should have thought about bringing one up with me, but I didn't, and I didn't feel like walking back downstairs to get it off my to be read pile. This wasn't a book on magic. Not everything had to be, and even the most dedicated witch had to unwind sometime. If not, they would go crazy, and if the council thought I was a danger just being a vampire and a witch, can you imagine what a crazy vampire witch would be like? This was a book I had picked for pleasure reading. An activity that I did every moment I could steal away from my studies, and just sat in my window reading.

Sitting there with Jennifer while the rest acted like teenagers around us struck me as funny, and I had to fight back a laugh. Here we were, the old fuddy-duddies, but yet, we didn't look more than a few years older than them.

Three chapters into this "Romance on the Bayou" novel that I once saw Mrs. Norton reading. I still hadn't figured out why she liked these things so much. Cheesy lines, flat and shallow characters that were borderline dumb, and a plot you could see where it was going on page one. I had tried a few of them before, and it didn't take long before I noticed the pattern. Woman hates man, there is an event that causes them to have to work together, and in the end the woman realizes she can't live without the man. That was formula one. Formula two was a woman is with someone else when her soulmate walks into her life. She frets over her situation, and in the end is with her soulmate while the other man vanishes, destroyed forever. Then there is the third formula, which is what this book was, and the type I hated most of all. It involved a naïve woman, a sophisticated man, and lots of wooing that she resisted even though she didn't want to. Of course, in the end she came around. There was something insulting about these characters, but I soldiered on.

I became so absorbed with picking this book apart piece by piece while I read it that I didn't even notice our approaching visitors until they sat down in the seats across from us. I looked up and saw Mr. Bolden sitting across from his wife. A confident smile danced across his face. Next to him, something I wasn't expecting. The menacing figure was gone, and in its place, a well-dressed, well-behaved, seemingly under control and rather attractive blonde teenager, and I wasn't the only who had noticed. The girl talk across the way had stopped, and the girl gazing had begun.

His pale complexion accentuated his high cheekbones, giving him an almost regal or noble look. The clothing he wore helped with that. Black slacks that fit like a glove around his muscular thighs and slim waist. A white shirt that hugged the triangular lines of his torso up to his wide shoulders. Even his posture added to the presence. It was upright and firm, even for a vampire. Both of his arms were lying on the arms of the chair, not loosely, almost like a frame that became one with the chair to hold him, or it, up.

"Evening Ladies," Mr. Bolden beamed.

"Evening Clayton," Jennifer responded, almost ignoring her husband.

"It's Clay ma'am. Just Clay," said a voice that no longer seethed. There was no grunting or even hints of restrained anger and hostilities in his words. It was a natural southern tone, deeper than my own, which I had adopted thanks to the continued exposure to my mother and Master Thomas. Nathan thought it was sexy, so of course I kept it up.

"Well, nice to meet you, Clay," she responded.

He turned his attention to me and regarded me with a long look. "And Larissa, I am so sorry about how I behaved earlier and that day down in your room. I wasn't... myself. I do apologize and hope that doesn't start us off on the wrong path." The apology seemed and felt genuine, and almost heartfelt. "I am feeling much better now, thanks to Mr. Bolden, and I doubt that will happen again."

"Don't worry about it, Clay. No hard feelings, and I am glad you are feeling much better," I said and attempted to hide the surprise in my voice, but I was thoroughly impressed. In just a few days Mr. Bolden had turned that animal into a human, and a rather charming human at that. "It is very nice to meet you," I said, figuring this was a better time for formal introductions than our last encounter. I reached forward, offering my hand.

Clay leaned forward, taking it. "And it is a pleasure to meet you." He held on to my hand and caressed it for several seconds before releasing it. His touch titillated me, both inside and out. I wasn't prepared for that, or for the feeling of three girls staring at me. I wouldn't hear the end of this anytime soon.

"So, how did this happen?" Jennifer asked.

"Well," Mr. Bolden started, "We just finally agreed to the terms and rules. Clay had a private hunt. Let's just say he has been refreshed spiritually and physically."

"I was in sad shape, if I do say so myself," Clay said very openly. "Just a shell of a person living on a diet of cold blood from dead animals I ran across. Real vile stuff. I would feel sicker after I fed than I did before, but I had to. It stopped the burning." Jennifer and I both nodded at that. "On top of that, I didn't have anyone there to help teach me how to live."

"Well, we are glad you are here. I assume my husband has given you the welcome to Coven Cove speech?"

"Yes ma'am. The whole lot. Magic building and all." Clay nodded.

"Good, and the rules?" she asked, with a scolding tone.

"Absolutely. Don't hurt anyone. Don't fight anyone. Go to class and learn everything. Feedings are on Fridays, and only in a designated area."

"Good." The pleasant Jennifer returned.

"We made a special exception to help heal the body. Spencer accompanied us, just in case."

Clay leaned forward and shook his head back and forth before his right hand came down to meet his brow. Then he sat up, exclaiming, "My oh my, I have seen a great many things in my life, but I ain't never seen a grown man turn into a large wolf right before my eyes. That had me scared so bad."

"It never gets old," I assured him.

"I understand you went toe to toe with him," Clay said, sending a little bit of shock through me. Both my and Jennifer's heads swung around toward Mr. Bolden, who sat there with the biggest *who-me* look on his face.

"In a way, yes, but that is not important." I fought the smile that threatened to sprout on my face. I wasn't proud of it. Well, not completely. It wasn't my finest moment, but it was a moment that I showed what I was and what I could do. "So how long have you..." coming out of my mouth, the question seemed rather forward and intrusive. That was not the first question anyone asked me. It wasn't even the second or the third. It was days, if not weeks, later. Though, I couldn't really answer them at that point, anyway. I didn't know.

"I guess right around three months," he said. "You could say this is all new to me. How about you?"

"About eighty years." I saw the surprise on his face. "Long story."

Off in the distance I heard Mike remark, "about eighty years long." I wasn't sure exactly when the boys had abandoned their movie. They were now all turned around, watching what Jennifer had called step two while the movie continued to play behind them.

"Come on over, everyone. Meet Clay." Mr. Bolden motioned for everyone to come on over and join us. "He doesn't bite."

With the looks I saw on Apryl and Pam's faces; it wasn't Clay I was worried about being a biter. Both had this look on their face. The look every teenage girl gets when a handsome new boy arrived in school, and like a scene out of every teenage movie, they swarmed over. I actually felt sorry for Clay. He sat back, trying to keep his space from the others, but kept his eyes on me. That didn't go unnoticed.

7

Clay didn't join us in our morning classes. Mr. Bolden didn't feel he was quite ready for mixed company yet, and he wanted to be cautious in his introduction to those with beating hearts. Especially with him being such a newborn. Jennifer told me he was even concerned about taking him out hunting, worried that his superior strength would be too much for him and Mr. Markinson together. That if he had a breath to hold, he would have held it during the entire trip. Clay behaved himself the whole time, much to the relief of both men.

I kind of imagined the process of introducing him to the others was kind of like introducing a new dog to a family. Though I doubted a leash would be involved. That might be appropriate if we were talking about Rob, Martin, or Dan. The thought of putting either of them on a leash made me giggle. You just have to walk him in and hope he doesn't growl or react to anyone. The question would be, how do you do it? How would you control nature's perfect hunter? By nature, we were strong, fast, and cunning. He would be too much for any one person to control as is. Have the burning take hold in him, and all bets were off if any of us, or all of us together, could grab and restrain him before he reached whoever his target was. I was told it usually took a week or more before anyone of us was ever introduced to the others. Well, everyone except me. Me, it was the day right after I turned back. I wonder why there was that level of trust.

I made a note to ask Jennifer later about how it worked, or really how they did it. Not that everything was about me, but I was more than a little curious. Why was I thrown into the pool with no real concerns? I also had a few ideas of my own about how to do it. My being both may give me an advantage no one else had. There were no doubts witches could defend themselves, but they may lack the speed to react fast enough. The same with the dog pack, though each of them would challenge me on that point. A little bit of ego, which was probably still bruised from the last time they challenged me, and a lot of animalistic machismo. I still had spent little time with any of the shapeshifters except Amy, but I had to assume Clay's speed might be a problem to them too. Mr. Helms had mentioned more than once, my natural abilities gave me an advantage if I could harness it, and I had. Now that I had my memories back and spells came more naturally, I could cast them faster than any of the others, even Mrs. Saxon. Not that we have ever had a duel. The idea of one was interesting. I already could out draw anyone else, even Mr. Helms and Mr. Demius. It wasn't even close. Most of the time, my attacks were on the way before they even knew it. That would help me react if Clay lost control and followed his impulses, but the idea I had didn't require that, just some ingenuity that anyone could muster. Or that was my theory. I would need a test subject to try it on first, just to see if it would work with someone tame before I tried it with Clay. Something to try on the deck tonight.

His lack of presence didn't keep him from being the talk of the classes, though. The fascination around our new guest even helped to bridge some of the divides that existed between the various groups. I wasn't sure if it was Laura's use of the word gorgeous or the word sophisticated that first got Tera's attention. Her continued description gathered more and more followers, and a few off looks from Mike, who didn't seem to be too pleased at her level of interest in our newest member. A reaction that was echoed by most of the guys.

The dog pack just ignored all the talk, and only Martin commented with his typical, "Great, another blood sucker." I gave him a warning filled glance, and he leaned back to the table. "Present company excluded," he said, and then he leaned in closer. "Look, we are always a little uncomfortable when one of you arrives. Not all vampires are as cool as you guys are. It's just a matter of time before one arrives that believes or harbors the old beliefs where we are enemies with each other. The history between our kinds hasn't been kind to either of us."

"Clay's a newborn. Just a few months now. I doubt he knows anything about any of that."

"Even worse," responded Martin with a sigh. "He's strong, and he knows it. I just hope he doesn't try to show it." He returned to his table just as Mrs. Saxon was calling class to order.

"So, what do you think of Clay?" Nathan asked.

"He's nice," I said, not really thinking much about my answer, and thinking more about getting my poetry book opened to the right page. While I remembered everything from the school I attended way back when, and spent a lot of time reading the classics over and over again with the Nortons, some of which I could now even recite if needed, poetry was the one thing I didn't have a lot of exposure to. There wasn't a single book of it on the bookshelves at the Norton's, so I needed to pay attention.

"So, he is nice?" Nathan responded. I could feel the warmth of his breath on the side of my face. I turned and met his gaze. He faced me; his head propped up on an arm with a goofy smile.

"Yep, nice," I said as I turned back to my book.

"Is that nice looking?" He prodded.

I turned to find him the same way he was just moments ago. He had yet to open his book. "Just nice." I pointed at the front of the classroom where his mother had started her lecture.

"From what I hear the others saying, he is gorgeous."

I jerked back in my seat. I knew that tone and wasn't in the mood. I wanted to pay attention in class and not have to deal with this, not now, and not really ever. It had to be nipped in the bud before it continued further. I turned slowly. He was still sitting there looking at me, head propped up.

"He is nice. That is it," I forcefully whispered. Then I glared at him to express my frustration in what I believe was happening. I prayed he got the message.

"The others seem to think he is really attractive." He didn't get the message. Not in the least. I didn't turn to face him this time. It was my turn to collapse down and prop my head up on an arm, an arm that blocked Nathan's view of my face.

"Drop it!" There was no whispering this time, and it drew the attention of everyone else, prompting them to turn around and stare. Even Mrs. Saxon had stopped her lecture and was looking back. I knew she was about to ask me something about what I had said. Maybe she thought I was telling her to drop it and expected me to explain why what she was saying was wrong. I greeted all the attention with a quick, "Sorry," and a wave of my hand. Slowly, everyone turned back around as Mrs. Saxon resumed her lecture.

Nathan didn't say another word for the rest of class. Something that both pleased and concerned me. The normal little comments, or little touches of my hand he did either on top of or under the table didn't occur. There was a space between us that I had probably inserted.

When class was over, there was an unusual migratory flow out of the classroom to the next class. Normally, the groups walked together. Not that things weren't cliquish, they were, but it was natural groupings. Vampires walked with vampires, witches walked with witches, werewolves and shapeshifters walked together most of the time, and I, the person who fit but didn't fit, walked with Nathan, the other person who didn't fit. Of course, that was by my own choice, and I wouldn't have it any other way.

Today, the balance of the world was off, way off. Like destroying the nature of things off. Witches and vampires congealed together into a single mass, walking out of the classroom. All talking. Talking, not trading barbs. The subject, of course, was Clay. There was a part of me that liked this. I was no longer the topic of the secret conversations. Now I was just, well, nothing, and that was simply fine with me.

Nathan and I waited for the mass of teen girls to move out the door before we made our exit. I was honestly afraid if we hadn't, they would have run us over. They were all so distracted; Gwen didn't even deliver her normal dirty look she always gave when she saw Nathan and me together. The closer we were, the dirtier the look. Now, well... just the thought made me giggle on the inside. Nathan was nothing to her anymore.

"This is going to get complicated," Jack whispered as he walked past.

8

"Any issues?" Mr. Demius asked.

Well, let's see. Gwen and I still don't get along well, or at all. I now know Mrs. Norton is alive, but I don't know if she is okay or where she is. Ms. Parrish is still not a fan. A raving lunatic old vampire still wants me, oh and my boyfriend is jealous of the new hot vampire that all the other girls are going nuts over. "No issues."

"So, Mr. St. Claire hasn't made any house calls?" a familiar voice asked from the darkness. He walked forward and as the shadows parted, he revealed himself. I wasn't sure why, but seeing Master Thomas was always a relief. Maybe it was because he appeared to be on my side. Maybe it was just his way. Very calm, loose, and laid back was his way. The diffuser of situations, the easer of tensions, and, as Gwen had noted a few times in her book of the council, he wasn't hard on the eyes. I just couldn't ever let Nathan know that.

"No sir. Not since I put the runes up."

"Good. I wasn't sure it would work," said Mr. Demius. He almost looked surprised. "Let's not celebrate quite yet though. It has only been one day. He may have not tried yet. Let's get started. We have a lot to cover."

"Will any other members of the council be joining us?" I asked, curious that Master Thomas was here, and even curiouser that no one else except Mr. Nevers had come since the last time the council had all gathered here when I returned from Virginia. None of the check-ins that I had imagined were going to be commonplace had occurred. That image of a child in foster care came into my head again.

Master Thomas hopped up on the center table in the first row of the classroom and threw his arms open in a grandiose move that looked like a Broadway actor waiting for the spotlight. "Nope. Just me." He hopped down and joined Mr. Demius and me at the front of the classroom. "It will probably be a long time before most of them venture here again. At least the troublesome ones. I am here because I have a real vested interest in you, Larissa."

"Really? Why?"

"You are the window to our past. A world long forgotten, and a world we still need. The witches nowadays label some of what you know, and are learning here, as dark magic. The name itself attaches a stigma to it that is just vile. It in itself defiles what it really is, true magic. Anyone can pull and push things, set things on fire, change what they look like. That's kid stuff. The stuff five-year-olds that are properly trained can do, but that is all they teach anymore. They ignore the true magic. The magic we were born to do. Unfortunately, much of it has been labeled as forbidden by the council... Not... Allowed... To... Be... Taught, and why? Because it allows someone to truly develop into who they are. Larissa, do you know where your true power comes from?"

"Focus," I said. It was the answer that had been beaten into my head since I had arrived. Come to think of it, my mother and father both beat it into my head too.

"Yes and no." Master Thomas turned to Mr. Demius. "Isn't that right?"

"Yes, it is," he answered, though he appeared to have become uninterested in our visitor and roamed around his classroom, straightening chairs, and waving away any dust that was on the tables. I had to wonder why he really needed a full classroom. Lisa and I were really his only students, and all of my work was after the official classes.

"Larissa, your true power comes from your family, and not all families are created equal. Some have more ability... no, that isn't how I want to say it. Some have a more powerful gift than others. What they teach now keeps everyone basically on even footing. Only a few of the spells and tricks they teach are things that not everyone can do, and that is how they now separate out the gifted from everyone else. A completely inadequate and biased method."

"And completely unnecessary," Mr. Demius interjected from several rows of tables back.

"Absolutely," Master Thomas agreed with a very animated nod of his head and a clapping of hands. "It holds everyone back. No one reaches their true potential. All for one reason, Larissa, would you like to guess what that reason is?"

I would have loved to, but to be honest, I didn't have a clue, and must have said that with my expression, because even if I wanted to, he didn't give me the chance to answer.

"Control. They set these rules to limit the potential of anyone else, protecting their families legacy on the council for generation after generation."

Luckily, the excitable man paused to breathe. That gave me just long enough to comprehend what he had just told me. It didn't take my brain long to remember the origins of the problem Mrs. Wintercrest had with me — well really my family. Knowing, and having lived through that, made what he proposed believable, and rather ironic. "So..." I started, but he interrupted me quickly.

"That's unfair, you say. Of course, it is. I could say I am a benefactor of that rule. I am the fourth generation on the council, but I feel I kind of earn my stripes with the work I do. I don't just sit up there, dress fancy and bathe in the surrounding mysticism and adoration." He smiled. "But plenty of them do. So yes, I am interested in your development. You... could change everything."

"But isn't that what they were concerned about?" I asked, remembering all too well the hell of those, um, discussions. I had barely recovered from the inquest. All the questions and accusations about me, and the Nortons, left more than a bitter taste in my mouth where the council was involved. It was poisonous. Mrs. Tenderschott told me to forgive and forget, and I was trying, I really was, but I also couldn't forget another comment she had made once before about the council. It made me feel really untrusting of them. Only one had broken through that feeling, and now I was standing here hearing him talk about doing exactly what the council accused, tried, and attempted to convict the Nortons of. And, I had just gotten used to my head not spinning.

"Absolutely." he crouched down a little and held his hands out toward me. "But let me lay it out for you. What they said was, they were concerned about vampires preparing you to become the ruler of the largest vampire coven in the land, and as a witch, potentially being a threat to their own positions. Now, they could have cared less about you taking out Jean St. Claire. But all that was just what they said, and we found truth was at the opposite end of the spectrum wasn't it? They were really concerned about you following your family's footsteps, and finally taking the role your mother or father should have taken. Add in the fact you would never die..." He let that hang there and stared deep into my black eyes. I wasn't sure what he would see. If he says understanding he would be wrong.

"You would rise to levels never seen before," Mr. Demius replied. A quick clap and point by Master Thomas marked that as the correct answer.

"Exactly. Now, what happens is all up to you. I just want to make sure you have the tools."

Again, there it was, and I would not let it go. "So, you want to groom me to be ready?" My choice of words was purposeful and appeared to hit both men with a direct shot.

"Not at all," shot Mr. Demius, who showed a renewed interest in the proceedings and rejoined Master Thomas and me at the front of the room.

"Absolutely not," added Master Thomas. "What your destiny will be is your own decision. You are free to do whatever you want with your life. I am," he pointed back at Mr. Demius. "We... are not here to tell you how to live your life. We can just help you discover who you are."

"Larissa, Master Thomas and I are the only ones that are familiar with the old ways. Mrs. Saxon has some knowledge, but as Master Thomas said, teaching of such is forbidden now. As such, her knowledge and ability in those matters is limited, and she would never take the risk."

"If it is forbidden, then won't you get in trouble teaching me?"

"Not at all. We are not the ones teaching you," Mr. Demius said.

Hearing that sent my head spinning around looking for another witch, or other council member. The shadow darkened corners were of my utmost curiosity. If they were there, they were hidden well, and very gifted at masking the sound of their own pulse. I only felt two there with me.

"Your mother already taught all this to you. We are just helping you remember it. Refreshing your memory as it would be."

"Oh," I exclaimed. It was both in surprise and then delight at the opportunity to further strengthen my memories of her.

"Larissa," Mr. Demius started and stepped in front of Master Thomas. "Remember our conversation yesterday about the importance of embracing your past? This is your past. You can't let the passage of time rob you of remembering and honoring your past."

Master Thomas hopped back up on top of one of the front tables again, and I saw Mr. Demius cringe. He had just cleaned that table, and I couldn't help but notice his gaze was directed right at the man's black soled shoes and the dusty footprints he left as he walked across the surface. I sent a light gust of air across the surface of the table, removing the prints and earning a "Thank you," from Mr. Demius.

"Larissa, this is your life." With that, Master Thomas wiped his hand across the air above his head. Dozens of flaming symbols appeared across the room, and to my amazement, I knew each one.

9

"So, Larissa, tell me about young Clayton."

"Not you too." I threw my hands up and looked at Mrs. Tenderschott in disbelief. A woman of her age, with cheeks flushed. What was going on in this place? Had she gotten into one of her own love potions?

"What? I hear things," she remarked back.

I still couldn't believe my ears or my eyes. All that was missing was a big colorful fan in her hand waving furiously to cool herself off. It was almost too much, bordering on, well, being uncomfortable. "He is nice," I said, downplaying it, just like I had with Nathan earlier, but for a completely different reason.

"Nice?" she asked.

"Nice." My black empty eyes tried to explain. "He seems polite, but still a little raw. Mr. Bolden is still working with him."

That was when she seemed to pull herself back together. She gathered the papers off of her desk into a stack. I glanced down at the stack and even craned my neck to try to see if any of the papers were mine, and if they were graded. "That will be you one day." She pointed her finger at me.

As she walked away to take the papers back to her residence, I gave a half-hearted, "Possibly." Not that I had really thought about it. I was just glad to be off the topic of Clayton. It didn't take more than a second before I realized I had walked right into another mess.

She stopped right at her residence door and spun around with a grin as big as Texas on her face. "So, you are considering a future here in the coven." The joy in her voice was palpable.

I throttled her back with, "It's just a possibility."

"Well, come on in and join me. Let's speak of such possibilities."

I followed her in, and even though it had been a while, a little chill still went down my spine as I sat down on the sofa. The same sofa I was on the first time Reginald Von Bell spoke to me during one of the Mrs. Tenderschott's attempts to find out who was following me. Each movement to settle on the cushion was a cautious movement with the tension of the last visit invading my muscles, robbing them of anything that resembled fluid movement. One by one each of my muscles relaxed on its own when it realized his voice would not speak to me. She had returned from the back rooms of her residence before I had settled all the way back. "You know, some have stayed and become a member of faculty here. Others stay active and stop by from time to time for special occasions like ascensions. I am sure Jennifer and Kevin would love the extra help."

My response was another non-committal, "Possibly." I was hoping she was going to drop it, but I knew better. All anyone around here seemed to talk about was the past or the future, and I found myself longing to enjoy my present. Things were pretty good, and I had moments I could push the concerns of my past into the past, and not worry about what questions and problems the future held.

"Have you given any thought to your future?"

At least I could until someone asked me a question about the future. "Yes," I admitted, and before my internal filter caught it, I blurted out. "And it seems others have too." That was something I had really attempted to fix, or tighten up. I doubted it had an off switch, but needed a little better control. Figuring it would be a good sign of maturity.

"Oh really? Are others trying to get you to stay around?"

"Stay, get married, maybe even have kids, and take over the council." I let it all fly. "Oh, and has there ever been a wedding in the coven itself? Jennifer couldn't remember ever hearing of one."

Either my list of all the proposed reasons I should stay, or the question shocked her. She was in the process of sitting down in the floral print chair across from me, but froze halfway down. Her eyes locked on me until her body eventually broke free of the shock and started down again. "I can't say I ever remember hearing of one," she stammered. "I take it Jennifer and you have talked about it?" Her rear finally hit the cushion.

"Some." Her eyes lit up at my reply. "But it is just talk," I quickly pointed out. I didn't need her running to any conclusions and start picking out my wedding gown for me. Especially when my mind hadn't even thought about the possibilities with any level of sincerity. "She wasn't the only one though," I added, somewhat subconsciously.

Mrs. Tenderschott returned a curious gaze, which I might imagine she would. "Nathan?" she asked directly.

"Yes and no," I answered, causing the curious look on her face to graduate to full on confusion. I knew there was no way I was getting out of there without explaining. "Not in so many words. Mostly indirectly. He made a few comments about what our life would be like at various ages."

The confusion evaporated right before my eyes. Replacing it was the warmth of a grandmother looking at her granddaughter. The dreams of happiness, love, and grandchildren danced across her face. "Young Nathan is rather smitten, it seems. Especially if he is thinking about your future together..."

"Hold up," I shook my hand to cut her off. "It's not like that."

"Oh, but it is," she interjected, returning the interruption favor. "I can see it when you both look at each other."

"You are right, it is that, but that's not what his comments were about." There I did it again. I confused her. "It's more concerns. When he is forty, what I am going to look like? What about when he is seventy?"

"Oh," she said grimly.

"Yep, that," I said in the same manner. We were two grim women – move over Brothers Grimm – sitting there with a problem that sucked the happiness that normally accompanied thoughts of Nathan right out of the room. That was why I forced these thoughts out of my mind as quickly as possible when they occurred. They still crept in without my permission from time to time just to give me that unasked for splash of icy water.

Both of her hands raised up and slapped down on her thighs, surprising me. After the impact, she sprung up, rather quickly for someone of her age. Of course, I was older and could jump about thirty feet straight up. "You have it in you to solve that problem," she said with a wink. I knew what she was talking about, and I wouldn't curse him to this. No way. Not that I had that bad of a life, if you took out that I was hunted, feared by humanity, had to kill and drink blood to survive, and had to stay in hiding for the rest of my life. The one plus, I would be hiding with Nathan, which actually sounded like heaven on earth. I was about to explain that to her when she raised her hand up and snapped. Now it was my turn to jump up from my seat.

"What do you think?" asked that attractive and very young teenage brunette dressed in a poodle skirt, white shirt, and saddle oxfords.

I was speechless, and that didn't happen often.

"You can be whatever age you want to be. Why not age yourself to match him through the years?" She twirled to model the skirt.

That was an option I hadn't considered. It was something I could do that other vampires couldn't, and it would last. Not that it would really change me, but the illusion was a form of glamour, and it would change what everyone saw when they looked at me, and wasn't that what matters? Appearances? Kind of like what I did for Amy when I helped her complete her costume, but a little more permanent. Perception was reality, and I could easily fool that. I felt a little silly not thinking of that on my own, and it actually gave me an idea of something to do later. "Well, that solved that, but it still leaves another problem."

She stopped her third twirl and looked at me mischievously. "Larissa, please tell me you and your mother had the talk."

"The talk?"

"Yes, THE talk." The mischievous grin grew as the syllables exited past her lips.

It hit me like a ton of embarrassing and uncomfortable bricks. "Yes," I said, then I quickly corrected it, "well no." She never did, and neither did Mrs. Norton. None of them did. It never came up.

"No. Oh god no. No one did, but that isn't it." I cringed to prepare myself for Mrs. Tenderschott to step in and give it to me herself. Eww.

"So, it's not about children?"

"No. Hell, I am not even sure if we can have any."

Hearing that sent Mrs. Tenderschott back to her seat. As she sat, she turned back to herself. "Have you talked to Jennifer about it?"

"It came up, and like in so many ways, I am a mystery. They have never known a couple between a human and a vampire, but that isn't it either."

"Then what is…" she collapsed back against the back of the chair. "Oh," she said woefully. "Oh. Dear," she said breathlessly. The color drained out of her face.

"No. Not that either," I gushed out to save her from the same heartbreaking, unavoidable reality that constantly invaded my thoughts. No matter how hard I worked to keep it out of my thoughts, it visited uninvited anytime it wanted to. This wasn't just a splash of cold water. It was throwing me into the bottom of an ice-covered lake. "It's Master Thomas, and the council."

"The council? They haven't been around lately. What are they bothering you about now?" She sounded irritated at the very mention of them.

"You are going to love this. It would appear my mother taught me a type of old magic that no one learns now, and it is actually forbidden to teach."

"Like what?" She sounded concerned, and the rosy color that was always present in her cheeks drained away right before my eyes.

"Well." I stood up. "Like this." I waved my hand across the air between us. The blazing symbols appeared just like both Master Thomas and Mr. Demius had done before in his classroom.

The sheer horror that crossed Mrs. Tenderschott's face even scared me. "Get rid of them!" she screamed, and then sprang up from her own chair, and rushed over to slam her door shut. When she turned, she admonished me, "Don't even display those again. You are right, that is forbidden. Nothing but trouble comes from those."

"Then you know what they are?" I let the symbols burn out in front of us.

"Absolutely, and it's best you do not discuss them with anyone else." She cut me a curt look as she crossed back to her chair.

"And you know why they are forbidden?"

She rubbed her face with her hands and looked up at the ceiling. I could feel her heart rate speed up and smelled the small beads of sweat that formed on her skin.

"Don't give me anything about it being dark and evil magic. Mr. Demius and Master Thomas already told me the difference, and they explained why."

"I know. I know," she said. Her hands waved in front of her face. "Larissa, you need to be careful with this. I can't warn you enough. This is one of those times you just need to go along with the rules, no matter how stupid they may seem."

"Why?" I interrupted. Her heart skipped a beat and there was an audible gasp when I asked.

"Just don't! I shouldn't have to explain it to you." She reached up and wiped her eyes. I couldn't see any tears, but just seeing the reaction struck me hard. I didn't expect this to upset her this badly. It was just a casual conversation. "If they really explained the true why to you, then you already know the answer to that question." There was another wiping of her eyes, and her left hand lingered a bit to rub the bridge of her nose. Signs of stress, her expression, and her body. I had seen all of them in films we studied in the Bolden's class the few times I was in there. "Haven't you had enough problems with the council?" The question was breathless.

"Yes, but that is the funny thing." Not that there was anything really funny about this. It was more ironic than anything.

"It's Master Thomas that is pushing me to learn it."

"What?" Her eyes sprung open. "He should know the price of teaching it."

"He isn't teaching me. Neither is Mr. Demius. My mother taught me. They are just helping me, remember?" I knew how stupid it sounded as soon as it exited my mouth. It sounded just as stupid as it did the first time they both tried to explain it to me that way, and it sounded just as stupid as the look Mrs. Tenderschott now gave me.

"That is rather convenient. Don't you think?"

"If you think that is fascinating, you will love this," I started, and watched her settle back in her chair. Most of the stress I saw in her expression was still there, but she appeared calmer. Which was good. If I knew her as well as I thought I did, this next part would make her explode. "Remember what we were talking about and how we got on this subject... my future?"

"Yes," she answered timidly.

"Master Thomas wants to help me remember so I can challenge for Council Supreme. He said I would be the only one who would have both the knowledge and ability to complete the four miracles, whatever that is."

"You have to be joking!"

"That is what I thought, too. The irony considering what I just had to clear my and the Norton's name of."

"Well, that, but also, it's not that simple. We do not elect these positions. It's almost like royal families. The same families are always on the council, and the act of changing who is the Council Supreme has led to actual wars between the covens, and these aren't just disagreements. I am talking an out-and-out war. Do you remember that time I called the council witch-hunters?"

"I do." I remembered it clearly and often wondered about it.

"That was just for anyone that broke simple rules, like learning something they shouldn't. What you are talking about now is a completely different matter. The hell they put witches through that break one of their precious rules would be a vacation compared to the life of torture they would put you through if you even tried."

"How bad?" I was curious.

"You really want to know?"

I nodded.

"Well, the simplest and most common is being made to serve one of the families. Basically, becoming their stooge, and it isn't just you. It's all future generations," she paused to regard me and then continued, "yea... um... That is the typical. Depending on the offense, they may forbid anyone from teaching your children the ways of witchcraft, ending your family's line there. But for something like you are talking about, it would be excommunication from all covens and forced to live in exile at best, and hunted for the remainder of your days at worst."

"So basically, the life of a vampire." I stated, not trying to be funny, but it appeared some of my natural sarcasm leaked into my voice.

"This is not a joking matter," she admonished. "Did you forget who your family was?" Her face puckered, like the cat that ate the canary. "After your last little issue with the council, I did some of my own reading on your family. One of the few families powerful enough, and respected enough, to have ever challenged for the council if they wanted to. If you tried, it wouldn't be dismissed as just a foolish gesture. It would be seen as a serious challenge." She leaned forward and pointed right at me. "This isn't playing with fire. This is playing with lightning, and you, Mr. Demius and Master Thomas should know better."

10

It took a little bit to calm Mrs. Tenderschott down. Bringing her back to the topic of Nathan Saxon did the trick. She had started planning our own wedding, and I didn't dare stop her. It put a smile on her face, which was better than the fearful looks the other topic had produced. Plus, not that I would ever admit it, it was kind of fun to think about, and it gave me a moment of levity and a reason to smile myself.

After I left, her words on the other topic returned, and I started wondering if I was being foolish even trying to remember what my mother had taught. If I was being dangerous, then Master Thomas and Mr. Demius were being downright reckless, and even treacherous when you consider how the council might view their involvement, technicality or not.

On the way out to the pool area to meet Nathan and Amy for our little time together, I paused at the door to the library for a second and considered going in and asking what books he had on the subject. I thought I could teach myself and finish what my mother had started, while telling Master Thomas and Mr. Demius I was no longer interested. This seemed like an amenable compromise, at least in my head. There was one detail I hadn't considered before my hand touched the door handle: the council. If they were looking, they could see everything I read in the library. I would be naïve to think that none of them were still checking in on me. There wasn't any doubt that Miss Roberts was. Her way to earn a few brownie points with Mrs. Wintercrest.

There was another concerning possibility. I was being set up. Just by letting Master Thomas and Mr. Demius help me, I could be playing right into the council's hands, once again proving their points, and now they would have two witnesses that were in high esteem. A thought that made me shudder. It was shocking how few people I really trusted. Not that I didn't have an abundance of reasons to be so untrusting.

When I joined the others up on the deck, I made sure to not follow my natural instinct and stay off to myself. That always drew the attention of the others. It would be a source of a dozen "what's wrong" type of questions, and frankly I was more than a little tired of being the center of all the pity, I mean attention. Hopefully, the curtain had closed on the Larissa show for the time being, if not for good. Luckily for me, there was another show in town. The Clay show was on full display, and it was an entertaining one, unlike the Greek tragedy of Larissa.

Clay was comfortable with us. Not shy, and willing to talk about almost anything. He immediately fit in with the guys, being a lover of every nature of sport, with football being his number one. Something he, Jeremy, and Mike spent more than a few hours talking about. Even Mr. Bolden got into the mix. Being older, he had seen more of the stars of yesteryear, many of whom he had seen play with his own eyes. They ate up each story and even started quizzing him on stats and the debate that could never be settled. Who was better? Insert the name of any player from thirty years ago and the name of any player now. The favorite of sports fans, and one I even heard Mr. Norton debate with himself, and sometimes the commentator on television, from time to time.

The girls, on the other hand, didn't contribute to the discussion. They were all right there in the front row, taking it all in, and drawing more than a few raised eyebrows from Jennifer, who kept her distance. Even I could see it, and I wondered if it was because of my age, and extra maturity, that I could see how they were all acting like smitten schoolgirls. I just hoped I didn't look as silly falling all over Nathan, but I had a feeling I had, and continued to from time to time. I may have been worse.

Even Pamela was getting involved in Clay auditions. That is what I started to call it after the first few hours. She was wearing make-up, something I hadn't seen on her face since I had arrived in the coven. Like Jack said earlier, this was going to get complicated.

He was easy on the eyes, but he was also easy to talk to. His open personality seemed to invite everyone to talk to him. A huge contrast to my first encounter with his seething expression. I couldn't believe he was the same person. I had to remember how Brad described himself for the first week or so, and even Mike said he was about as rough. I didn't remember ever being like that. I hoped it was because the Nortons knew how to take care of me and my needs, and not a case of my not remembering something. Looking at him now, I felt he was going to be able to acclimate to the others very soon. Of course, he wasn't being tested by our presence. There were no pulses up here to knock on his temptations, but it wasn't stretching it to say I was impressed with the progress.

I knew I couldn't mention that to Nathan, who had already shown signs of jealousy, though I didn't understand why. He still hadn't met *the* Clay and hadn't heard me talk about him at all. He was just going on what the others were saying, and I had to hear all about it after we finished reading the first Nancy Drew book with Amy. She read most of it aloud. Then we had a lively debate about whether Nancy had ever dated either of the Hardy boys. A preposterous point asserted by Nathan from behind a large grin. He wasn't grinning that much when he asked about Clay, and again all I could say was, "he seemed nice." It didn't help that later in the afternoon Mike had seen Nathan in the gym and mentioned Clay and how he and I talked a lot. I used Mike's own words against Nathan and emphasized *talked*. He kept on and I stopped short of telling him that jealousy wasn't very becoming, though there was a benefit. I couldn't remember the last time he kissed me the way he did when we said good night.

"So, how about it? Larissa, are you in?" I heard it but had no clue what Mike was talking about.

"What?" My mind was elsewhere.

"Dodgeball. Day after tomorrow, out in the clearing in the woods."

"I'm not sure," I said, still trying to pull my head to the here and now.

"Come on. It will be fun," added Clay. He seemed excited, and I could understand why. He had been trapped in the coven since he arrived. This gave him an opportunity to get out safely.

"We are going to invite Rob and Martin so we can have six per side." That addition Mr. Bolden made, and the look he exchanged with me, told me everything I needed to know about this invite. If there was anyone that could defend themselves against us, it would be Rob and Martin. Doug was still young. This was a test, and a controlled test at that, to see how Clay did in mixed company.

"Sounds like fun. I will try to make it." The look I received from both Clay and Mr. Bolden seemed to be disappointed in my non-committal reply. I felt I needed to explain. "I have a session with Mr. Demius."

"Even on the weekend?" Apryl asked in disbelief.

"Yes, even on the weekend. Every day. There is still a lot they need to catch me up on."

"Secret witch stuff," remarked Laura.

My black eyes rolled at hearing her say that. That was a path I didn't want to go down again. I had heard it a few times since I wouldn't report back to them as a spy about Lisa's ascension ceremony. Mostly when they knew I had gone down to the witch's floor for something. They wouldn't buy that it was just like our floor, which it was. So, I made up that there were black cats all over the place, every room had a cauldron, and they all rode brooms. Not that anyone bought it and saw through my sarcasm. That didn't stop Apryl from commenting on what Gwen could do with her broomstick. I was about to remark back for them to knock it off when I noticed the shock on Clay's face. That was when I remembered, I hadn't shared my other half to him, and if no one else told him... well, the black cat just jumped out of the bag and flew all around the deck on a broom.

"Yes, Clay. I am a witch and a vampire."

Every head on the deck turned toward him to watch his next reaction. I wasn't sure what to expect, but I was ready for anything.

"You're a witch? But how?" he stuttered. The smooth southern voice that seemed to swoon the others was now struggling to sound coherent.

"Yes, and it's a long story." Without even intending to, I had just given Clay an invitation to come down and talk to me for the rest of the night. There were more than a few looks from the girls when he moved next to where I was seated. A few of those looks rivaled the worst Gwen could give.

I explained to him my family's history, which he seemed completely fascinated with. I even owned up to my age. It was something I needed to do, just like I eventually had to with Tera so we would stop the - have you ever been to—game. The Louisiana and Mississippi those two remembered was not at all the same place that I remembered. There was no Super Dome, or even big Mardi Gras festivals, which seemed now to just turn into an excuse to come to town and drink for a few days. The New Orleans I remembered was a world focused on the ports, cotton, tobacco, sugar cane, and the Mississippi River. We were still close enough to the river to hear the whistles on the steamships and paddle-wheels as they traveled up and down it. As far as I knew, there was probably an interstate running through our farm now.

After explaining my life history, in as short a version as possible, I hoped things would return to normal. Why, oh why, did I have hope anymore? I should have learned long ago what happened to those. Clay moved even closer and had even more questions. The result? More dirty looks from the others. I had a few looks myself, but those were for help, and I sent them Jennifer's way. Her response, just a smile. I knew why, and I understood it. The more Clay talked with someone, the more comfortable he would feel, helping him progress in getting acclimated, but that didn't help me at the moment. I was already not in the mood to talk, especially on the topic Clay wanted to talk about - me. My best defense, turn every question about me into a question about him, and not only was he more than willing to talk about himself. I learned something; maybe I wasn't the most tragic story in the place.

Clay was turned just two months back. He told me he remembered the attack clearly, something I didn't until just recently. It was early evening, and he was walking home after seeing a movie with his friends, Tim Barber and Sean Burns. Clay even remembered the movie, a title I made a note to check out later. "Summer Slaughter" sounded like something that would be at the top of my list. Maybe something to watch with Nathan and the dog pack. He said he was alone when something hit him, knocking him to the ground and dragged him into a dark alley.

"If I had to say, not that I have ever been hit by a bus, which is what the impact felt like, and I never want to feel that again. I am sure it broke a few bones," was the description he gave for how it started.

After that, everyone in ear shot could relate to his tale. The sting of the bite, which was then followed by the excruciating burn. It only got worse from there. If there was a bright spot to Clay's story, the turning itself only took a few hours and not days, like it did for most. He went into the story of his first hunt right after. I felt my heart break as he spoke of the guilt he felt for the life he took. That was something I couldn't relate to. My first hunt was an animal, the same with every hunt thereafter. He was in Starkville. Not a large city, but a city none the less, where the most common creature was man. Jeremy and Mike both nodded along while hearing a story that mirrored their own very closely. I think I was the only one who noticed Apryl as she slinked away a little further during that portion of his story. There was a look on her face, but it wasn't one of disgust. No pinched lips or glares in Clay's direction. She was looking everywhere but at anyone and appeared solemn. I had to wonder if there was a similar story there for her. Not that I was going to pry. That wouldn't do any good and if she ever wanted to talk about it, she would.

What I wasn't prepared for was the next detail, which, if I had to be honest, might be the most heartbreaking of anyone in the coven. Not that I knew everyone's complete backstory. I just couldn't imagine anything worse. After his hunt, he didn't know what to do with himself. He had been left alone to fend for himself and to figure out what his place was in the world now. Neither was a task he was prepared for. So, what did he do? The only thing he knew to do, he headed home. He got as far as opening the door before he let it shut and ran away because of the pain and agony that ran through him when he smelled the blood coursing through the veins of those inside.

He believed they heard him open the door. Why else would they come out to the porch and call his name? Something he could hear clearly from behind the garage where he stayed for three days. On the fourth day, he heard his father come out to the garage, get in the car, and leave. Clay believed he may have been going out to look for him. Later that night, he returned and lingered in the garage. He was just on the other side of the wall from Clay, which was way too close. The temptation. The feeling. The draw of the smell set him off, and as Clay said, he did something that wasn't him. He called for his dad and waited at the back door of the garage. It happened in a flash, and it was over before Clay even knew what had happened. He sat there, crying as loud as he could; his clothes were soaked with his father's blood. His cries were too loud and lured his mother outside. The next thing Clay remembered, he was running across the field behind their home, and through town, soaked in the blood of two parents, with nothing but the shattered remnants of what he called a home behind him.

I tried to help him understand it wasn't him, it was this... but then I realized I didn't know what to even call it. Our condition? Our urges? Our life? As a newborn, he didn't stand a chance. The primal call inside of him was going to be answered whether or not he wanted to. It was just tragic that his parents had to be the ones to be there.

"You can't blame yourself," I said again, trying my best to help him understand. Jennifer had moved beside him. Uncomfortable expressions dominated the circle that had gathered. Apryl still hadn't joined the close group, but that didn't mean she wasn't paying attention from afar.

"I know," Clay agreed, but I wasn't convinced he really believed it. His voice withered away, and his gaze dropped to the floor. Not even the support of all of us could help wash it away, or even dilute it, and I think all of us knew that. Some more than others. It was just going to take time, and it was important that he understood it.

In one last attempt to comfort him, something I think I felt I needed to do more than maybe he needed it due to how heartbreaking his story was, I reached over to rub his shoulder. His hand reached up and caught mine before I did, and there it was again. Not the pleasant, but uncomfortable sensation that brought me alive inside. This was the harsh, malicious intent feeling from before that. I tried to pull away but couldn't. His grip was too tight on my hand. It was almost painfully tight. Another yank, and nothing. When I yanked again, his head jerked up and there it was again. That chilling blank stare, and the seething evil grin.

"Clay." I yanked again. He didn't give, and instead yanked me out of my chair close to him. This brought both Jennifer and Mr. Bolden to their feet. The others all jumped in their chairs. His death grip was becoming painful, but I believe the stare I was now inches from was even more disturbing; it was personal.

"Clay. Let go of Larissa," Jennifer calmly requested. She inched toward him. His head jerked in her direction, but my reprieve from his glare was only momentary as he turned back toward me.

I stopped playing and pulled back with all I had this time, but his other hand reached up and grabbed me by the back of my head and forced me closer to his. "Clay, let me go. You're hurting me." I demanded. His response, a very slow shake of his head to the negative and one word, "You."

That was it. I wasn't doing this anymore. I gave him everything my other side had and threw him back through the chair with a bright flash. He bounced across the deck a little harder than I expected him to. What I did to Jack was nothing compared to this. Mr. Bolden ran after him, and I stood up. "Clay, I am so sorry!"

When he sat up, I could see he had returned. The hate filled look was gone. One of pure confusion replaced it.

11

"Hey Mom." I greeted my mother walking into the kitchen, where she always was when I came for a visit. There was a theoretical question on my mind at that moment about if her being trapped in the kitchen was her fault or my fault, but that would have to wait for another time. There was another topic I needed to discuss.

"Hi, sweetie." She hugged me and rubbed my arms quickly in what I knew was an attempt to warm me up.

Now that I could do this on my own, I had been visiting my mother every few days. Sometimes to just say hello and talk, much like I believe I would have done once I had grown up and had a family of my own, if life hadn't hung a left out of the normal lane. Other times I had specific questions that I needed her help or opinion on. Today was a question visit. I wasn't here for her to help me with a spell or to go back over some of the things she had taught me when I was younger. She was my private tutor that neither Mr. Demius nor Master Thomas knew about.

"So how is that man of yours?" she asked, putting a cup of coffee down in front of me on the kitchen table. Her hair was put up in a tight bun, and her smile was as radiant as ever.

"He is good," I said, and felt myself smile on the inside. This was one of the few snippets of normal life I experienced. I told my mother about Nathan a few visits ago. To my mother, I guess I still looked human. She said she could tell I was in love with him, that the glow I had when I talked about him gave me away. When I returned to the coven, I felt weepy. Not because of Nathan, or anything my mother did. There was a loss. The realization of one of any hundreds of true mother daughter moments I had missed out on. At least I had a way to still experience some of them and was going to make sure I did that as often as possible. "I do have a question for you, mom, and it's about you."

"Me?" she asked, stunned over the top of her coffee cup before taking a sip.

"Yes you. I read you were very respected and even considered for a seat on the council. Is that true?"

"Possibly," she said coyly before taking a second sip. After which she put her cup down on the table and straightened up in her chair. She regarded me with a rather interested look. "Why the interest in the council?"

"I was just curious. You know, learning more about my family, and all." I said with as straight as a poker face as I could, but there was something about this woman's eyes. She had a superpower, and its name was parenthood. That came with certain innate abilities. The two most widely known was the guilt machine, the ability to make a child feel guilty instantly, and the look. The look was a powerful one that rivaled any magic I knew, and it came in many forms. Just the feel of it could make a child squirm, just like I was now. I called this look the inquisition. She knew I was holding something back and intended to find out. Its secondary effect froze you. No matter what you did, you couldn't escape. Now was no different.

"Curious about the council, I see. It's an odd thing for someone to be curious about."

"Not really. I just heard some things."

She ratcheted up her look a few notches on the intensity meter before leaning forward against the table, bringing it closer to me. "Actually, it is, considering I never told anyone about the offer. Only your father and a few members of the council knew." She leaned against the table and propped herself up on her elbow. "You've talked to the council." First there was an accusatory finger tracing an invisible circle in front of my face. Then she leaned back with a prideful grin. "The council has approached my daughter. How about that?" She almost cackled.

Yep, I had been, but not in the way she believed, and let's not even get into my first experience with the council. That was a complete and utter travesty, and not something I could even broach with my mother. Not now, not ever. She would need some background information that I would not provide. What she didn't know wouldn't hurt her. She didn't need to know that, and she also didn't need to know that they approached me in a way that appeared to be a coup attempt on the council supreme herself. "Two members have reached out to me with some interest. They are helping me to refine my craft."

My mother leapt to her feet and rushed around the table and practically lifted me out of my chair into a hug. Then she swung me around the kitchen in a dance where she was the leader, and I was the partner who had no choice. It only took a few turns before I gladly joined in to share the joy of this moment with my mother, even if there were circumstances that cast an enormous shadow over it. "I am so proud of you," she crowed while holding me at arm's length. She didn't have to say it. I could see it clearly in the gleam in her eye.

"Thank you."

She pulled me for another hug, and again didn't make a comment on how cold I felt. Probably her own pride was enough to warm us both.

"I do have a question about it," I said with my face against her ear. She let go of the embrace and took me by hand back over to the table, where I sat, but she remained standing. That joyful look plastered on her face. "Why did you say no?"

"Larissa, my saying no shouldn't have any bearing on your decision. You have your own path to follow."

"I know that, but I am curious. From what I heard, they really wanted you to be a member. Why did you turn it down?" I gave in to her illusion that it was someone on the council that had told me all these details, and not history books.

She looked deep in thought, but never lost that gleam in her eye. "It just wasn't for me," she said plainly.

"But why?" I was probably starting to sound like a young child that asks their parent why after every explanation.

"It just wasn't. I wanted to be a mother to my lovely daughter," her hand reached down and caressed the side of my cheek, "and I wanted to teach here at the Orleans' Coven. Being on the council is a huge time commitment. It would have taken away from both of those, and that was not something I wanted to do. So, I politely declined the offer, but agreed to advise when needed."

Where I was expecting some kind of deep political struggle-based rationale, I received something that made complete sense. So much sense I had to wonder if it was really as simple as that. What my mother had taught me wasn't forbidden at that point, and I seriously doubted that something as old as the council only recently started becoming political and full of power mongering families. I already knew that was the case. "Mom, do you remember a family with the last name Wintercrest?"

"Absolutely. They were prominent members of our coven. Why do you ask?"

Here it goes. Most everything I had told my mother I had left little bits of detail out. "A member of their family is now the supreme and I hear there was a little issue where they were bypassed for a seat on the council for you, and that is why they left the coven."

"Ryan is the supreme?" She sat down across from me. The gleam gone, and curiosity took its place.

"Not him. Another member of the family. Mrs. Wintercrest. I don't know her first name."

This agitated my mother to no end. Her hands fidgeted with one another on the table, and she bit her bottom lip. Something I used to do but didn't dare do it now. "Odd, she wasn't that..." she mumbled, and then righted herself. "They are a fine family, and you need to remember she is the supreme. You are there to assist and serve," she said timidly. "She will be lucky to have you on her council." Then she paused again, and again that curious look planted itself right on her face. "Why am I getting the feeling you have a few reservations about joining the council?"

A few reservations? Try a couple hundred, and again ignoring that the offer was really more of an attempted coup by other members of the council, all in the name of some noble cause of restoring witches to what they used to be. Hell, with all I have read and heard about my mother, she would probably approve and want to take up arms right next to me, but she couldn't, and I feared if she knew, it would only frighten her. She would be trapped here, worried about me, and unable to do anything about it. That sounded like the darkest depths of hell, and I didn't want to do that to her. And again, there was no reason to. She couldn't help me. "Just weighing all the options."

"That is important to do. Especially if you are thinking of any sort of life or family with that man of yours. I am sure he understands that time commitment of the council, but I would make sure you two talk about it. Communication is key to any successful relationship." That gleam was back in her eye, along with a lopsided smile.

I was absolutely sure Nathan didn't understand the time commitment of the council. He didn't even understand what the council was, other than a sore spot in many of our arguments. Communication was key in relationships, just not on that topic. Of course, my mother would expect he would know all about this stuff. I didn't tell her that he was a human. One of the many details I have left out. Really, the only one I had left out where Nathan was concerned. She knew everything. She was my mother. "Speaking of that, how did you know dad was the one?"

"Oh Larissa," cooed my mother.

12

"What no new guy yet?"

I looked right at Nathan, eyes narrowed and intense. There it was again. A hint of jealousy that robbed his voice of the pleasant sound that was music to my ears. Now it sounded like a kid first learning to play the violin, scratchy and irritating.

My reply was nothing. I ignored him and he didn't seem to appreciate it much, it was something I hadn't done before. I felt a few gentle nudges by his arm while we were supposed to be paying attention to Mr. Markinson's lecture. I was, Nathan clearly wasn't.

When class was over, I went to get up, but he quickly grabbed my hand. He knew better than to try to hold me back, but I also knew this wasn't the time to remind him of that and did what any girl who was having a little issue with her boyfriend would do. Just like Juliet when Romeo grabbed her hand. I feigned no interest at first, and then I turned back to him.

"What?" he asked, as if he was clueless about the source of the look I gave him. I hoped he was now the one playing a game.

"You know precisely what," I barked, just like millions of women before me.

"I don't have a bloody clue. I just asked a question."

"Actually, you asked two to be accurate." I yanked my hand away to finish my point. "Let me give you those answers. First, no, Clay is not ready yet. He still has a lot to deal with, but you wouldn't understand. It's a vampire thing." Normally I would have never said that to Nathan because I really want him to think of me as a girl, a woman, and not any of the other things I was, but at this moment, I didn't care, and if it carried a little sting with it, then all the better. "Second, knock it off. Jealousy doesn't become you." I turned and headed toward the door, but I knew Nathan wasn't far behind me. I wanted to see what his next move was. Hopefully, for his sake, it was an apology.

Just as expected, I felt a hand on my shoulder, but the voice that accompanied it was a surprise. "Larissa, got a second?" Jack's voice sounded concerned.

"Of course." I followed Jack down the hall but looked back at the door. I left Nathan standing there watching as we walked a few doors down. I looped my arm through Jack's for added impact. Oh, to be able to feel thoughts like Jack.

"You okay?" Jack asked when we stopped.

"Yea, fine. Why?" I was a little irked at Nathan, but the intensity in Jack's face was more than just that.

"I felt it last night. Just like the times before. Is St. Claire still coming to you?"

"No. Not in several nights." I haven't felt him even try since I put the runes up in my room. I had thought it would only protect me in there, but it appeared to have a much larger radius of protection, not that I was complaining. Mr. Demius said how far it would stretch would depend on my own strength.

Jack looked at me confused. "Are you sure? I felt just like that time a few weeks ago. It woke me up from a sound sleep."

"I'm sure." I was about to ask him if he was just having a nightmare when I realized what it might have been. "Wait, about what time was this?"

"Just before five this morning."

That could be it. I mean, there wasn't a clock up on the roof with us, but it seemed to line up right compared to when the sun came up. "I think I know what you felt. We had an issue with Clay around that time. He seemed to relapse. It was bad."

"Maybe that was it." He seemed unconvinced. "It sure felt like a visit."

"If I remember what Mrs. Saxon told me once. You feel the intensity, right?"

Jack nodded.

"Well, Clay was definitely intense. He was seething and about to attack. I had to throw him across the deck to calm him down. You probably felt his rage."

"I guess."

"I am fine, and he is fine. Nothing to worry about," I reassured him.

"So, no issues with St. Claire recently though?"

"Nah, Mr. Demius and one of the council members showed me a trick to block him." I didn't dare to get into the symbols, runes, and all that with Jack. Way too risky. Not that I felt Jack would rat me out. The fewer people who knew, the better, for their own good.

"Okay." Jack seemed to ease up in his concern a little. Maybe, hopefully, he believed what I told him. There was no reason not to. It had to be it. Maybe it was a combination of Clay's anger, and the rest of our fear combined. There was plenty of fear going around up there. I know I felt it. "Just remember, if you have any problems, you can talk to me."

"I know."

He looked down the hall, and my gaze followed his. Nathan was standing no more than ten feet from us, waiting, and looking none too happy. Jack sighed. I would have if I could have.

"See you in class," Jack said before he departed.

He walked right past Nathan, and there was a terse exchange between the two.

"Jack."

"Nate."

Here we go again. I walked toward Nathan with no intention of stopping. I needed to get to class, but as much as I tried to hold my tongue, my natural tendencies got the better of me. "You're unbelievable."

"Thanks." His arrogant tone almost caused me to turn around. Almost. I increased my pace, and he hurried to catch up.

"That wasn't a compliment, just so you know."

"I figured. What did I do now?"

Jealousy and playing dumb were two traits that were not attractive on my boyfriend. I was sure there were others, and I was sure I could work past them. My feelings for him were stronger than that, and I had to remember his age. I had to fight the urge to remind him of his age, and just how immature he was acting. Nothing good would have come from that. He was just an eighteen-year-old boy, and both traits were common among that age. Even his little show of machismo as Jack walked by, like a male lion staking his claim, and as much as I wanted to remind him I wasn't anyone's property, I had to accept the fact that I enjoyed being his. Like Jennifer had told me, I needed to pick my battles, and I already had one going on. "First Clay, and now Jack, again!"

"Jack?" The denial in his voice was stronger than the odor of his own blood, which was quite strong. Not that I felt out of control, but it didn't go unnoticed that today was a Friday.

"Yes, Jack," I finally stopped my march. Not because I wanted to turn and face him in reaction to anything he said. I wanted this finished here, and now, before we got any closer to the class where others might see us. There was no way I was going to put on a dramatic showing like this in front of Gwen. As far as she was concerned, life with Nathan and me was perfect. No chinks in the armor of our relationship. No opportunities for her to try to pry an opening in. I knew Nathan would never let her in any way, but that wouldn't stop her from trying. Even if it was just to get a rise out of me. "I saw the way you were looking at us when we were talking, and then how you acted when he walked past you. I am not going through this again with you about him. There is nothing there. Just a friendship, and... as I already explained to you, he understands me probably better than I do myself at times."

Nathan made every attempt to blow off what I just said. His quick huff and looking around told me all I needed to know. He was trying to find a comeback to defend himself. I just wanted him to drop it. "What did he need to talk to you about?"

I debated with myself whether to tell him or just dig at him a bit more and say it was a witch thing, but since I had already played the vampire card, it might backfire on me. "An emotional outburst woke him up this morning."

His jaw dropped momentarily and then tensed up. He was about to ask a question, but I stopped him before he could. "It wasn't mine.... Well, not entirely mine. We had an issue with Clay last night. He lost control and became filled with rage. I think what he felt was that, and the fear the rest of us felt until we had him under control, but just like you jumped to a conclusion, he jumped to the same one and wanted to ask. That was all. Now, can you let it go and stop acting so jealous?" I stepped forward and got up on my toes and kissed him. "You don't have any reason to be. Okay?"

His hand gripped mine again, but this time it wasn't to restrain me. "Yep." He kissed me again, and when I pulled away to head to class, he pulled me back. I expected a second, third kiss, and I wouldn't have resisted it, but he never leaned in. "Tomorrow night's my mother's tree decorating party. Would you do me the honor?"

13

I wasn't watching the clock, per se, but I was eager to leave my extra training session, which had gone a little long. It wasn't a bad-long, but it was a long-long, we normally spent maybe two hours, sometimes a little more. Today's session was now over four hours, and we wasted none of the time. Mr. Demius was handling my "training" by himself today. Master Thomas didn't join us, and other than the first day, Mr. Nevers hadn't returned. Something told me, though, Mr. Demius liked it this way. Just us. He did his best work, even if he wasn't really teaching me anything, just helping me recall, and then suggesting ways I could use it. What I learned today was game changing in so many ways.

I still wasn't sure I completely understood the enormity of what he told me, and then demonstrated. It was contrary to everything Mrs. Saxon, Mrs. Tenderschott, and Mr. Helms taught. Their lesson about magic was all about its structure. Knowing the right recipes for a potion. Knowing the right words for a spell. All what he called a leash to hold us back from what we truly were. Witches were nature's most wonderful creatures. We were the only ones that could wield all the powers of nature itself. We were agents of both change and chaos. The one truth in our world was there were no rules. The spells they are teaching are starter spells, and most believe that is all there was. Mr. Demius called that the great fallacy spread by the council to control us. The possibilities of what each of us could do were endless.

For the better part of an hour, he showed off, combining different symbols and abilities in ways I never imagined were possible. I approached the symbols and what my mother taught as singular abilities, one after another, where instead they were building blocks to unlock really anything. After his demonstration ended, he sat me down at the front table and explained what he felt really should be the lesson we should be taught, though he commented it wasn't because of the leash. It was a responsibility. While a witch with proper training had the ability to do anything they could imagine, the real power came from knowing when to and when not to. When he started down that road, my mind went back to what happened just a few days ago, and I asked, "like the baby duck?"

"Yes, we can create life, but we shouldn't. We must be responsible with our abilities." He was serious in his delivery, but not grim. That came next. "There are those that are not responsible. I know there is a stigma around the dark arts as being evil and wrong. The same with the old magic that your mother taught you. In truth, there is no such thing as good or evil magic, but there is right and wrong, and that is related to what you do with it. There are those who are not responsible in their usages of it. They live outside of the council's reach, and are part of an unspoken but very real war."

I wanted to ask about that last part. Was there really a war? But that was a question that never had a chance to reach my lips before Mr. Demius dropped the real load of bricks on me. It seems there was something much worse than a war going on in our world.

"The council has made a grave mistake by not talking about those rogue elements of our world. They should be used as examples to teach responsibility, and right and wrong. Instead, they use limits on what we teach to ensure that if someone is a bad apple, they don't know enough to cause serious issues. The danger in that is we are just a few years away from losing who we are. No one will remain who knows true magic, how to truly be a witch. A good witch. A responsible witch. You are a good person, so that is the kind of witch you will be. That is why what we do here is so important. You can be the one to correct the course we are on, and bring us, all of us, back to who we were."

Mr. Demius filled the next two hours yelling out odd requests, and me working to find the right combination to fulfill them. Some were as simple as performing the trick right there. Others were more like a spelling bee, having to recite the combination out loud. There was a lot more to this world than what he called "hand magic."

I left his classroom a little awestruck and more than a little intimidated. I thought I was just being groomed to challenge for council supreme. As daunting as that aspiration was, it seemed small and insignificant now. The reality was beyond anything I could fathom. If only Gwen knew that the future of witches depended on me. Hell, even I was uneasy about that.

Even sitting there with Amy in my lap reading "The Hidden Staircase," I had her reading much of it, the enormity of what I had just been told wasn't far from my mind. My distraction caused me to forget to turn the page a few times, only to be reminded by the sweetest voice in the world, "Larissa, you can turn the page."

With each reminder, I turned it quickly and gave a quick, "Sorry." I planted a kiss on the top of her head to beg for forgiveness. Nathan noticed and gave me a questioning look each time it happened. A line of questioning was no doubt in my future.

When it was time for her to head in for bedtime, or what it really was on Friday nights–time to head in so she didn't have to face what vampires really did, I held on a little longer. I know Mr. Demius and Master Thomas had an expectation of what my future needed to be, but I couldn't help feeling that this was the future I wanted. I only hoped there was a way to have both.

"Can she come with us to the tree decorating?" I witch-whispered to Nathan. This being my first time, I wasn't sure if there were any rules, and with how I was feeling about things if my request was against the rules, I was going to break it.

"Of course. She can come. I'll even pick her up," Nathan replied.

"For what?" the angelic girl looked up at me and asked.

"We are decorating the tree in the entry for Christmas tomorrow night. It's a big party."

The word Christmas hadn't left my mouth before her eyes and mouth shot open. I felt her body tense up, and then both of her hands clapped together. "A Christmas tree? I've never seen one before."

A single tear crept from the corner of my eye, and my voice cracked, "Well, you will tomorrow." My arms wrapped around her, and I had to remind myself not to crush her. I think even Ms. Parrish heard the exchange. Her normally stonelike expression showed cracks.

She went in after our normal exchange of hugs and I sat there and watched her disappear behind the door. I wouldn't be lying if I said much of my happiness left with her. Across from me was the source for the remaining portion and he was looking at me, concerned. I reached out and wiped the tear away. "It hurts to know she hasn't even seen a Christmas tree." It did. It hurt to my core to think that little girl never experienced Christmas. Her life was spent in a cage, and those gypsies didn't have the decency to at least give her that joy.

"I know. It does me too. We are going to fix that this year, big time."

"Yep," I agreed while choking back another round of tears.

"Is there something else wrong? You seemed to be somewhere else earlier."

I had lost track of how many times I promised myself that I wouldn't lie to Nathan, only to do just that. What I was about to do wasn't really as much of a lie as it was an omission. "I'm fine," I said, and then feigned exhaustion. "Mr. Demius just really put it to me today. There is a lot to learn." Please don't ask like what. Please don't ask like what. Whew, saved by the vampires.

Apryl and Laura emerged out the door, and it hadn't shut yet before Mike and Brad exited, leading a steady progression of the rest of them with Steve and Stan. Nathan was pushing up from his chair when the last of them appeared. He had made a habit of excusing himself and clearing out before the festivities occurred. Not that he would know what was going on. All the bloody events happened deep in the woods. I think just being around when we set off is a reminder of what we are, and he prefers to think of us as people. I know that is how he prefers to think of me. The last to emerge was Mr. Bolden and our newest member. Lucky guy, he was hunting for the second time in a week, not a treat he should get used to, but it was a good idea to get him on the same feeding schedule with the rest of us. It would make his adjustment easier.

Nathan's gaze followed him as he passed. There was a quick point in Clay's direction and a whispered, "is that him?" Which was really a stupid question. Who else would it be?

I nodded and mouthed, "Yep, now go."

Nathan finally did after he waited and watched Clay for a few seconds. When Clay said, "Hi Larissa," Nathan walked around the table, going behind it away from Clay, to give me a hug and a kiss that took a little longer than normal. Not that I minded, but I wasn't stupid. That was a statement, and it wasn't for me. He finally went in. Mr. Bolden reminded us of the rules, and we all headed out.

14

After the hunt, Mr. Bolden announced that Clay would be joining everyone at Mrs. Saxon's tree decorating party. He felt Clay had progressed far enough, and with the extra feeding, he would have enough control to take this step. He also mentioned several times, that it was a perfect opportunity to see how things go. No better way to test a newborn's self-control like throwing him in a room with the entire coven. I had a feeling Jennifer, and her husband, wouldn't be far from Clay the entire night just in case.

I spent most of the day pumping Apryl and Laura for information about the tree decorating party. I didn't know what to expect or have any idea what to wear. What they described seemed to be part fairytale and part high-school prom. While both told me what they wore the previous year, they spent more time telling me what Gwen wore. Hearing about her pink chiffon and sequined dress didn't surprise me. What else would it be. Apryl made sure to add in how low cut the top was, and how she knew it was for Nathan's benefit, whose arm she hung on all night no matter how many times he tried to get away. Luckily for him, I will be there to protect him this year.

My old memories of my parents' parties interfered with my own search. Their holiday parties were some of the grandest events I had ever seen. We decorated the whole house with green holly, mistletoe, red flowers, and velvety ribbons. As far as I was concerned, velvet was the official fabric of the season. Everything was covered in it, including me. I remembered it being a little scratchy. One year I asked if I could try green, but my mother told me no. They were always red, either knee length with white tights, or a full dress that was ankle length right down to my black patent buckle flats. What was a certainty, I was not wearing anything like that this year. Eliminating that one possibility didn't bring me any closer to the final decision.

It needed to be stunning. That much was for sure. I wanted to take Nathan's breath away. Yet a great irony was in my way. The magical closet I stood in front of was showing me a big bunch of nada. There were dresses hanging in there, loads of them, but they were just dresses. Not *the* dress. Of course, the closet was showing me what my mind thought of, which made me doubt my qualification to select the dress. My style was more jeans and t-shirts. I hadn't worn a dress like this since, well... the red-velvet dress with black patent shoes. There were several versions of that dress hanging in the closet, and there was no way in hell I was going to grab those, not after I heard what Gwen wore last year. This had to top that. Not that it was a competition.

I flopped back in surrender on my bed, hoping the magical closet would bail me out. A quick glance in its direction showed no change. I let out a scream and kicked the air.

"Larissa! Are you okay?" Jennifer screamed from the other side of the door.

"Come on in."

I didn't have to ask twice. She came through in an instant and she looked all around the room. "What happened?"

"I'm fine. I'm fine. Nothing is wrong." I said, feeling a little embarrassed. "The only thing wrong is that." I pointed at the closet and let my head fall back on the bed.

It started as a snicker that progressed to a giggle before exploding into a chuckle. I let it continue for a bit, but was growing close to giving Jennifer something to stop laughing about, though I had to admit I saw the humor in it too. Here I was, a witch and an immortal vampire, and I was being foiled by not knowing what to wear to a Christmas party. "This one isn't too bad."

She was snickering before I lifted my head off the bed to look. There it was, another version of the red velvet dress that I wore when I was eight. A quick flip of my wrist set it aflame causing it to disappear from sight.

"I take it that is a no."

"I have never dressed up like this before, except when I was a little girl, and that horrible cotillion dress." In a blink every dress was now a poofy light blue dress with a hoop skirt. Damn that magic closet. "No!"

The snicker returned, and Jennifer tried to stifle it while pulling out one of the offensive dresses. "This is very Gone with the Wind."

What a wonderful idea. Another flick of the wrist sent it flying off the hanger, along with everything else in the closet. The red velvet beasts replaced them.

"What do you want to wear?"

If looks could kill, Jennifer would be six feet under after one I gave her.

"Right." She diverted her eyes from me and went back to staring at the closet which wasn't helping. "Well, have you thought about a little black dress? They are classic and timeless."

I looked up as she pulled out several choices of that timeless classic. They were nice, better than the red velvet, but nothing wowed me, and if it didn't wow me, well then I knew it wouldn't deliver the reaction I wanted. "Nah, needs a little something." I just didn't know what.

"More glamour, or maybe something a little sexier." She pulled two out of the closet. The first was better, but the second brought me to my feet. It was almost perfect, when I grabbed the hanger from Jennifer, a slit ran up the side of it, and the neckline plunged a little further than it already was. We both exchanged a look. That was a at least a good start.

After a few more alterations Jennifer left to get ready herself. She offered to walk down with me, but I had other plans. My plan needed a grand entrance. One worthy of Gwen's disgust. So, I waited for everyone else to leave our floor and then made my way to the door where with a single finger I drew the symbol of the all seeing eye. The sign burned in front of me, and the door, wall, and floor became transparent allowing me to watch everyone gather downstairs around the tree.

I searched the crowd for the only one that mattered, but found myself distracted by the decorations that had appeared since I last came up those stairs. The snow that had been falling for over a month had picked up, covering the branches of the tree in a magical dusting. Green garland grew around the railing of the stairs. A family of tasteful snowmen, not the kind we created up on the roof, moved across the snow-covered floor acting like servers carrying trays of cookies, cakes, and drinks. I was actually jealous I didn't eat. Just seeing it there, I could almost taste the cider. A couple of deer, probably reindeer, walked around. And the twinkle of lights were everywhere. Walls, stairwell, doors, and some places you couldn't see the source.

It wasn't long before I saw who I was waiting on. If I thought Nathan looked good in a swimsuit, seeing him in a black suit and tie was a whole other level. He was suave, and debonair. Move over James Bond. Nathan Saxon was here, and he was licensed to kill my heart. Which would have been pounding a million beats a minute if it still beat. He rounded tree after waiting for one of the snowmen to cross in front of his path. When he stepped past the tree, I heard myself squeal. Amy looked like an angel, in of all things, a red velvet dress, white tights, and black patent shoes. Nathan was leading her wide-eyed around the tree. It was perfect, and the perfect time to make my appearance, I just had one more trick to perform before I walked through the door. Mrs. Tenderschott would be owed a great thanks if this worked.

I ducked back in my room for just a second, snapped my fingers, and took what was supposed to be a quick glance in the mirror, but it lasted a lot longer. The shock of what I did was more than I expected, and I had to force myself to hold it together. After one more slight alteration I worked up the nerve to walk out and down the stairs. Well sort of. I thought I had the nerve, but my hand missed the door handle twice. I was distracted and scared all at the same time. When I caught it the third time and gave it a turn, I told myself it is now or never, and stepped out on to the landing. Most were downstairs talking and didn't notice me at first, and now I was fine with that. My original vision had all eyes, especially Nathan's on me as I made a statement, but now I would have rather snuck down without being noticed. Of course, as I have learned multiple times, what I wanted didn't really happen often.

A few loud gasps announced my presence on the stairs, and the eyes of everyone else followed. Jennifer knew what dress I was going to wear, but I hadn't told her, or anyone else, of my other surprise. I hadn't even told Mrs. Tenderschott who gave me the idea. She was just as stunned as the others. Nathan appeared to be lost for words, as he stood at the bottom of the stairs waiting on me. In the middle of the silence that had now overtaken the setting, a small voice asked, "Larissa, is that you?"

I descended down the rest of the stairs and bent down to give Amy the answer. "Yes Amy. It's me. The real me." The young girl looked right into my big blue eyes set inside the rosy flesh of my face. Both of her arms latched around my neck and hugged me tight. When she let go, I stood up with everyone still gawking in my direction, and faced Nathan. "Hi."

"Wow. What happened?" He was breathless when he asked, and I don't believe his eyes had blinked since they caught the first sight of me on the stairs.

"This is what I used to look like, back before. Do you approve?"

"Uh yea," he said, but still hadn't blinked or moved. I was the one to make the first move and grabbed his free hand. Amy had laid claim to his other hand again. With that, some of the others started milling about again. We did the same. Well, I did. Nathan and Amy both couldn't take their eyes off me, and at one point I switched and moved over to Amy, so she was holding both Nathan and my hands. I pointed out the tree to her and explained that we were going to decorate it. Not that I knew how that would work. As far as I knew decorations might sprout on the tree while we all watched. I was grabbing her a few cookies from the snowman that passed by when Jennifer passed by.

"And I thought the dress was going to wow them."

I just smiled, but that was then I saw a scowl coming in my direction, and it wasn't from Gwen, and it wasn't alone. It had friends.

"Here you go," I said as I handed the cookies to Amy. I leaned over to Nathan, "Be right back."

I made my way to the source of the scowl, or make that scowls. There they were, a group of vampires sitting there dressed like the kids too cool for the prom. All the girls were dressed to the nines, and Brad, but Mike had forgotten to put on his bow tie and didn't even try to tuck in his shirt. Jeremy had opted for a plaid jacket.

"Well, well... I see you didn't drink your vial," sniped Laura. A single finger pointed at my vial that hung around my neck like a red ruby.

"Of course not, plus it wouldn't work anyway," I responded knowing exactly what she was referring to. "This is just a little magic."

"Tired of being one of us?" asked Apryl. There was an acidic tone to her question, and it burned.

"Absolutely not. Just something I wanted to do for tonight. For Nathan, and maybe a little of a shot at Gwen." I added the last bit to see if I could turn Apryl's frown around.

That was when the most shocking comment found its way into the conversation. Mike, of all people, Mister macho, the least sensitive of anyone here, something Laura had complained to me about more than once, stepped forward and put his hand on my shoulder. He had a pleasant look on his face. "I get it. You needed to show Nathan if there is a future, you can actually grow old together."

I nodded. That was a big part of it, but I also wanted him to see me, the me I was before, and after Mrs. Tenderschott gave me the idea, I couldn't think of a better time to unveil it.

I saw the expression on Laura's face change. She wasn't smiling, but she wasn't upset either. Pamela walked up and gave me a quick hug and kiss on the cheek as she passed by to join the party, but not before she gleefully announced. "Yep, she is still cold."

Laura and Mike were the next to go rejoin the festivities. Then Brad and Jeremy, leaving Apryl there in the corner with me. I stepped closer. "Please don't think I am turning my back on you or anyone. It's just something I wanted to show Nathan. I am still me; nothing changes that."

"I understand, just sometimes I think you enjoy being a witch more than a vampire, like it makes you feel more normal, and… well," she looked around the room, "I guess it makes me jealous that you have that escape."

Normal? Being a witch, in my opinion, took me further away from anything that resembled normal. I hadn't shared with any of them everything Mr. Demius and Master Thomas were working with me on, and definitely not the why. Nothing about it felt normal, though I wasn't sure if I would know what normal was if it bit me. I thought my life with the Nortons was normal. We seemed like just a normal every day, run-of-the-mill family if you ignored the fact that we were vampires. "Please don't think being part witch brings me anywhere closer to normal. It's far from it."

I watched as Apryl glanced over in the direction of Gwen, and then she smirked. "Point made." We both laughed.

"It was just something I needed to show Nathan."

"I know. I hadn't thought about it before Mike said something. He will keep getting older while you stay like you are. So, one day you will be kissing an eighty-year-old man. Just eww. That would be like making out with a grandfather." Apryl looked over my shoulder in Nathan's direction, and remarked "But, he might be a hot grandfather."

I looked back at him and had to agree. Nathan noticed both of us looking at him and waved at us sheepishly, causing us both to laugh again. Then Apryl headed off to join the others and I went back to join Nathan and Amy. I had a curiosity I needed to have answered.

"So how does this decorating thing work? Do they just appear or something?"

"Nah, we use traditional decorations for that." He pointed at a table in the corner with boxes stacked on top of it. "Now how they get up on the tree, is another matter. I do that the old-fashioned way, but some of the others choose to do it with more flair."

"Huh," I faked a moment of thought and then announced to both Nathan and Amy, "It will be the traditional way for me as well." That appeared to please Nathan, and Amy clapped. Though I wasn't sure she even knew what she was clapping about. She had already told us she had never seen a Christmas tree. Her happiness just seemed to be a constant state thanks to festive surroundings, and it was infectious. Not even the apprehension I felt when I saw Mr. Bolden escorting Clay down the stairs could dampen my spirit.

Our new arrival made an entrance, and Mr. Bolden led him around to make the introductions. Clay appeared to be handling things quite well. Not that I really expected any problems. I was more curious how he would do with all the new faces. It can be rather overwhelming.

"So that's him?" I heard Nathan ask from behind me. My first impulse was to say duh and remind him that he already asked that, but I resisted and said nothing, not wanting to encourage or start off any show of jealousy Nathan may have been working up. I had hoped I had ended all that yesterday.

When Mr. Bolden and Clay made it around to us, he proceeded with the introductions. "Clay, this is Nathan Saxon, and you know Larissa." I felt a hand grip me tightly around my waist.

"Nice to meet you," Nathan said. His voice sounded deeper than I ever remembered. I rolled my magically blue eyes, but Nathan could see them from behind me. There was a tug on my dress, and I looked down.

"Clay, this is Amy O'Neil." I directed his eyes down to the little girl that had a handful of my dress.

"Well, hello there," he said and bent down in front of her.

"Hi," she said, and then she partially hid behind me. You would think the girl would be used to the sight of a vampire's black eyes with all the time I had spent with her, but her reaction was the same as the time I was a pop-up vampire.

Clay stood up remorsefully.

"She is shy at first," I explained. It was as good of an excuse as any.

"It's not that. She reminds me of my little cousin. They are about the same age." I could see the hurt in his face and hear it in his words. After a few moments, he moved on to meet the others, but it didn't take long before his two escorts for the night, Apryl, and Laura quickly swarmed him. Mike made his objection known and quickly removed Laura from the situation. She only looked mildly perturbed until she caught the intense look Mike was giving her. It was animalistic. One of ownership, and she quickly snuggled up next to him and appeared to be happy about it.

That left a side, and I watched wondering if Pam would make her move, but she appeared to be happy dancing with Jeremy to the seasonal music that played. That was a pairing I hadn't expected to see, but in hindsight it worked. Both had similar low-key personalities.

Who swooped into the empty spot was predictable. The pink gowned queen-B didn't wait until Laura moved more than a few steps away from Clay before she walked over and introduced herself. Daggers shot from Apryl's eyes, and Jack crossed behind me and remarked, "Complicated."

He walked by hand in hand with Tera. Again, not something I saw coming, but I also couldn't tell if this was just accompanying one another or something more. Then a smirk crossed just before a light giggle escaped from my lips. "What?" Nathan asked.

"Nothing." I raised a hand to stifle another giggle while I wondered if I had started something in this place.

"You almost look alive," Martin said as he gave me a big hug.

"You still smell like a dog." He ignored me and turned his attention to Amy.

"So that is the new one?" snarled Rob. "There is something wrong with him. He smells dirty." He walked right past us and weaved through the crowd that now included all of the instructors, including Ms. Parrish and Mr. Helms. When he reached Clay, they exchanged a look and Rob circled around him and appeared to sniff the air behind him, and then held his nose.

"Ignore him," Martin said. "Well kind of. There is something about him. It makes me uncomfortable."

Two clinks on a glass cut off the music and brought everyone's attention to Mrs. Saxon standing there at the tree. She looked as elegant as ever in a sequin covered red dress with white gloves.

"Thank you. You all look so wonderful, and there is no better way to start this magical season than in the company of family and friends, and to me we are all family. This is a tradition here in this coven that goes back to the start. Every year this tree sprouts in the same spot after Thanksgiving and growing to full maturity by Christmas before moving on with the arrival of the new year, then next year it starts all over but stronger than the year before. Much like this coven. A continuous cycle, one after another, and each learning and growing from the previous generation. It is our obligation, and our gift, to lay the groundwork for a better place for the future generation, and part of that is the celebration of our traditions and expanding them. The annual tree decorating is one of those traditions that started with the first members of our coven, and like everyone before us, we continue that tradition while adding our own touch that we can build on next year. I present this year's ornament." Mrs. Saxon held out her white glove covered hands and the air around them sparkled. Then slowly a ball made of snow appeared. Leaves of gold sprouted from the top. After it hovered there for all to see, it flew across to the tree where it hung on a branch in the dead center of the tree. I guessed she wasn't doing her decorating the traditional way. "Everyone jump in, there are plenty of decorations to go around." She motioned toward the table, and the music began again.

A few moved toward the table and started pulling out the ornaments. There was no way I was going to just stand there and watch. I had a mission, and nothing would stop me. I grabbed Amy's hand and rushed her over to the table. Her eyes were wide saucers looking at all the shiny balls and strings of glittery objects.

"Well don't just look at them. Grab one and we can put it on the tree."

"Grab a couple," suggested Lisa. She picked up two shiny red balls and shoved them in Amy's hands.

"Now what?" she wondered aloud dangling one of the ornaments from her hand.

"Well, you hang them on the tree, silly." I walked her over to the tree making sure to position her close to a branch. "See the hooks in the top?"

"Uh huh."

"Use that to hang it on the branch right there." I pointed to an area close to the end where the needles parted exposing the branch. She reached the ornament out and placed it right where I showed her. When she let it go, the hook settled on the branch and hung there reflecting the twinkling lights that were all around. Once she did one, she was eager to hang the second and we found a second branch just for that one. We made several more trips back and forth between the ornaments and the tree before Nathan stepped in and took his turn helping Amy. He lifted her up so she could place decorations on higher branches. Watching him lift her up, with smiles across both of their faces, put more than a smile on mine. I was watching a dream. One I had had multiple times.

"And why aren't you decorating the tree?"

"Oh, I will, just enjoying something else for a moment," I said to Clay. I didn't feel I needed to explain myself and wasn't in the mood to even go there. I was literally in a moment of bliss, something I didn't experience often and just wanted to have this chance, and no one was going to take it away from me. Too late.

Nathan saw Clay standing next to me, and I watched as his expression changed. He was holding up a squealing joyful child as she helped Tera hang a long line of glittery gold balls, but he was stewing on the inside. As soon as Amy was back on the ground, Nathan let Tera take her and made a beeline straight for me. I knew what was about to happen, and I wasn't in the mood for it. This was a joyful occasion, and there was no way I was going to let Nathan's jealousy spoil it.

I walked forward and met him halfway and did something I once told myself I was never going to do to Nathan, and this time it wasn't about lying to him. When I reached him, I grabbed his hand and planted a deep thought in his mind using compulsion. Without question, he took my hand and the two of us walked back to Amy and the tree where the three of us hung ornaments with our friends.

"Ouch," exclaimed Tera.

"You okay?" Marcia asked.

"Yep, I just..." Tera didn't have to finish it. I and six others in the room knew exactly what happened. The smell was overwhelming. "... cut my finger on one of the hooks."

"Clay no!" I heard Jennifer scream from across the room. Before I could turn, he was already rushing through the crowd throwing people out of the way heading for Tera. Mike and Jeremy tried to grab him, but he shed them like empty bags of potatoes. Mr. Bolden was on the way, but I didn't believe he would reach him in time. I was closest, but even then, I wasn't sure I would make it there. Tera never even saw him coming, it was all happening so fast. She hadn't even started to move out of the way. I had another option, one I had thought of earlier, where the distance between us wouldn't matter. I pulled up my hands in front of me and then pushed toward his path and whispered a sorry to Tera in case this didn't work.

Clay slammed across the room and into the wall. Right then I put my plan in motion and watched his reaction. I moved my hand in his direction and a shimmer surrounded him and then disappeared. First there was confusion. He was still reacting to the thirst he felt, but it didn't feel the source anymore. It was unguided and searching.

Everyone else watched me as I walked closer to the corner I pushed him into. He calmed down and stood still. My experiment had worked. I knew I could make him think he was some place else. In this instance, he was standing in a forest of majestic trees with a cool night breeze blowing over him. What I wasn't completely sure of was whether I could block out that impulse.

"Is he okay?" Jennifer asked.

"He thinks he is somewhere else. I am going to keep him there until you get him upstairs." Mr. Bolden walked forward and entered the bubble I created. He looked around, now exposed to the illusion Clay was. He walked him through the woods and up a hill, which was really the stairs, and back into the coven after a feeding. To me that seemed like the most logical illusion to create to help Clay. Once he was behind the door, I let it go.

15

"Is he okay?"

"He's kicking himself," responded Jennifer. From where I sat, that was exactly what it looked like. The jovial Clay we had seen the night before was now sitting alone all by himself at the other end of our roof top deck. His head dropped down at the end of his neck. His hands alternated from holding his head up, to making frustrated passes through his hair, and at times even gripping full handfuls and yanking.

That kind of loss-of-control was something I had never personally experienced, and the fact the smell of Tera's blood didn't even faze me had to be because of my age. Right after Clay was handled, I saw Pam and Mike excuse themselves, and Jeremy followed. Though the others stayed, it didn't take a genius to notice everyone except me kept their distance until she went to get cleaned up. It was true, I smelled it. Its metallic scent was unmistakable, but nothing stirred. I even walked over with a napkin for her to wrap around her finger. Clay was a newborn, and Mr. Bolden said he didn't stand a chance. Even with it just being a single drop of blood caused by the hook on a Christmas ornament.

"He will get over it. It takes a while to gain control over it," Jennifer added.

"Maybe someone should talk to him."

"Kevin did after he brought him back upstairs. He explained to him it wasn't his fault, which it wasn't, and he even told him not to feel guilty about it, but you know..."

We both said in unison, "when someone tells you not to feel guilty you will." Damn those suggestions that sneak into your damaged psyche and twist all around. Just like being told not to be nervous about something.

There was another two handfuls of blonde hair. "I think maybe I should," I said.

Jennifer looked back in his direction and remarked, "Probably not a bad idea for someone to talk to him before he goes bald." I stood up and started, but she grabbed my elbow lightly. "Just keep it simple. Remember what he has been through. His experiences are different than yours, so you might not understand. That is something you need to always remember when handling someone new."

At first, I thought this was a warning, and an odd one at that, but then it clicked, and I looked down at her. "Training?"

She smiled. "Think of it as your first lesson, but I think you will be a natural."

I wasn't about to admit I had doubts in that as I walked over toward Clay. Add on to it the suspicion that Jennifer might be watching, evaluating, and that frog in my throat went from tadpole to full sized toad in about twenty steps. By the time I sat down on the chair across from Clay, I felt it might evolve into a something even larger, causing a quick swallow to try to discard whatever it was. "Clay," I croaked.

He didn't look up, but his hands paused on their way back through his hair again. "Are you okay?" I knew it was a dumb question, but it was a logical opening.

"No," he mumbled, still looking down at the deck floor.

"Understandable." I adjusted my posture and sat up straight. Convey confidence, and you will feel it. That's what they say isn't it? "That wasn't something you could control. It's not your fault, at all."

"It was the same with my parents." His hands completed another path through his hair and gave two handfuls a good, frustrated yank.

"Look it's primal and takes years to learn how to control it. Your mind wasn't in control then, or tonight. Nature overrode everything else."

"I know." His head tilted up, but not far enough for me to see his face. "That feeling of just being along for the ride. Like someone or something else had the wheel, and all I could do was watch while that feeling ate at me whole. I knew inside there was only one way to make it stop, and at that same time I knew I couldn't let it happen, but I was helpless to stop it. It's just... just... how did you deal with it?"

Clay's head finally emerged the rest of the way up, and his hands brushed the hair away from his face. I could see the pain of the evening as plain as day. Red streaks lined down his face, probably from his own fingers as he tried to claw the memory out. I used to think you couldn't see emotion in our black eyes. I was wrong. I could see every gut wrenching feeling he had in his while they searched mine for answers, and that was a big problem.

Luckily, a wise vampire had given me the answer before I walked over, because thinking back on my own experiences, I found I couldn't really relate. I never remember feeling what Clay described. "It's not about how I handled it. The experience is different for everyone, and how you deal with it is as unique as you are. It just takes time." Feeling rather proud of how I conveyed that, I decided to branch out on my own and broach new ground. "What is important is you understand this wasn't your fault, and it wasn't anything you could have stopped, at least not yet. In time you will learn how."

The young man didn't seem to be comforted by my words, and instead looked away in anguish. "It was just that smell. I was already feeling a little on edge being around that many... you know?"

"You could feel and hear it moving, couldn't you?"

"Like the drum beat of my favorite song," he looked back at me, and there was a connection in his eyes. "It was all around me, but I was forcing myself to focus on ignoring it," then Clay stopped, and his hands gripped the back of his head again. "Oh God!" his voice exclaimed loudly. I looked toward the others, and they were all looking in our direction. I waved them off.

"What is it? Clay, talk to me, please?" I leaned forward placing a comforting hand on his shoulder. I was no longer acting how I felt Jennifer would want me to, or expect me to. This was the general concern for another human being. It was hard seeing anyone, even someone I barely knew, in so much pain.

"That was the first time they all met me," he mumbled. He let go of his head and sat up. "I wanted to make a good impression."

It was a memorable one for sure, but I couldn't tell him that. He felt bad enough as it was, and like Jennifer said, everyone's experiences were different. This wasn't something I could relate to. Not in the least. So, I channeled my best inner therapist, and with a mild amount of jealousy for what Jack could do, I assured him. "Don't worry about that. You will find that people here are not only ready for anything but also used to anything. It comes with what goes on around this place. They won't bat an eye." I wasn't quite ready to tell him about how we all had to fight off a few vampires in the grand entry on my account. They all still accepted me after that. Well, not all, but I think it would be safe to say Gwen tolerated me. A story would help, though. Something real to help him see past his current embarrassment and frustration and realize this too will pass and, most importantly, things will be okay. There just wasn't anything. My past, on that level, had been rather normal and mundane. The Nortons had made it that way, and only now, after seeing Clay and knowing some of the back stories of my friends, did I begin to appreciate what they went through to make it that way. There was one story that might work. "We all make our own splash. My first time out around everyone, I attacked Jack."

"The boy witch?" asked Clay, and I held back the chuckle hearing it termed that way. I was sure Jack wouldn't appreciate that description, but I filed it away for a time it might be useful. He got more jabs at me than I got at him. Now I had something.

"Yes, him. I was forgiven and now we are all friends, especially Jack."

The tension melted out of Clay's body, and he sat the rest of the way back. A little jerk of his head sent his long hair flipping out of his face, and a hint of a smile emerged. "So, you really attacked Jack? Did he cut himself too?"

I cringed at hearing those questions. My issue with Jack was a completely different animal than what Clay went through tonight. If the two issues were fires, Clay's was a three-alarm fire, and mine with Jack was just a match. They weren't really on par with each other, but it was all I had to go with. For a fleeting moment, I did consider using a little consumption trick to help him move past this, but that would only be temporary. There was no magic that would help him in the long run, just good old talking, mentoring, counseling, and time were the only ways to go here.

"Not exactly. He said something, and I sent him flying across the pool downstairs," I sheepishly explained. He looked on as if he were expecting more, and I quickly added, "But, in my defense, I didn't know I was a witch then. I thought all vampires could do that, and it only happened for me when I lost control of my temper."

"That's it?" Clay sounded rather annoyed, and I would have been too if the roles were reversed. I needed to save this and resisted looking at Jennifer to see if she was paying attention. I hoped she wasn't.

"I know. It's not the same, but just one of many examples of what happens around here."

Clay let out a huff, a remnant reaction from his past human days.

"Look, Mr. Bolden explained to you about the charmed doors, right?"

He nodded.

"And he said why they are like that, right?"

There was another nod, followed quickly again by a sense of relief that prompted a quick look up at the moonlight sky. "To protect us and others while we are adjusting and learning to control ourselves."

"Right, and remember, the doors aren't just charmed against us. They block anyone that doesn't belong on that floor, also protecting us from the others, like the werewolves and the witches. We aren't the only ones that go through an adjustment period." I gave him a little smile and a wink. Hoping he would let go of things and just accept it as part of his adjustment period. "Today was just an extreme test, and it even bothered some of the others enough that they had to leave after you did."

He seemed to get it, and relaxed even further, even slumping his shoulders. An odd move for a vampire. Of course, he hasn't been like us that long and it could be another hold over from before. Though I, and others, found that our posture change was almost immediate. There was no tiring of our back anymore, causing us to slump. Clay, on the other hand seemed to still have the posture of a human. "Did the smell bother you?"

"No, and there is no secret I can tell you to help either, in case you were going to ask. It just takes time. Remember my age. Now I smell it, but it doesn't faze me. You will be like that too one day. I believe in you."

Clay stood up and stepped toward me. "Well Miss Dubois, I thank you for the kind words, and might I add, you don't look that bad for your age." There was a flirtatious hint to his already rather southern tone.

I hesitated at first and dipped back into something I told myself I wouldn't do again. Not because it upset Nathan or broke any promise. It was more a matter of taste. With a quick apology to Vivien Leigh, I let it rip. "Well sir, I declare." My right hand fanned myself before I held it out toward him, and in a scene right out of the old Antebellum, he took it and helped me to my feet. I was feeling rather proud of myself, pulling him out of his funk, and I had every intention of walking him back over to the others, where the power of the group could help him recover even better. In my mind, others would come forward and talk to him, share stories, and further help him understand that this is just part of the process of being who we are, but Clay was full of surprises.

"Miss Dubois, it's such a beautiful night and such a beautiful song. Would you do me the honors?"

I hadn't even noticed the song that was playing. It was "Lady" by Styx. Brad's choice of music for the night. I didn't give it the second, or third, thought I should have before I accepted and held my arms up like I had for Todd Grainger so many years ago. Clay knew exactly what to do and took my hand with his and placed his flat palm against the small of my back. Almost like someone who had some ballroom dancing experience. Maybe something his mother had shown him before, or may I even think, some lessons somewhere in his past.

It was elegant, gliding along the deck to the song. The source of what should have been my second thought, Nathan, far from my mind. I wasn't doing anything wrong. Nothing in the least, though I was sure he wouldn't see it that way, but he wouldn't ever know, and even if he did, he needed to grow out of that immature jealousy phase. The sources of the third thought I should have given this glared a hole in my back. After our dance was done, I would make up for it by suggesting he rejoin the group and letting the others fawn over him and get their turns.

Dennis DeYoung was starting the chorus again when I noticed a change in the feeling of his touch. It was colder than normal, and the pressure was firmer, almost grabbing at me. My eyes found Clay's. There was no change there. The same pleasant smile rested upon his face. It was the most relaxed I had seen him all night, but as the feeling of the touch changed, the realization of what it was crept in. By the second refrain of that chorus, the surrounding night dripped away, and I knew what was going on. Another stressful night had compromised me and opened the door. My thoughts went to the runes. Mr. Demius said over time they lose a little. Right after this dance, I would excuse myself to go reapply them. I forced myself to keep up with Clay's movements, letting him move me around the deck. When he changed into the gaunt pale face of Jean St. Claire, a chill ran down my spine, and his hands dug into me more. I wanted to pull away, but I was afraid that if I did, I would pull away in the real world too, causing a scene.

"You look lovely tonight, Larissa, the spitting image of your mother," said a voice that wasn't Clay's. I knew it all too well. I knew that chill it produced well, too. Doing the best I could to ignore it, I listened to the song, hoping that would bring the deck and my dance partner back into focus, but I was faced with another surprise. The string quartet that was playing now wasn't Styx. I was now in a grand ballroom complete with marble floors, with the partner from hell.

"It doesn't have to be this way. The life I could offer you is beyond your wildest imagination." This was new.

His grip on me was like a steel trap. I pulled back a little, but couldn't break free. I was hesitant to pull back even harder to not startle Clay.

"We would be the perfect union. Me and you. The perfect combination of God's most amazing creatures."

The leap my head made into what he meant made me gag. He couldn't be proposing what I thought he was. Of course, he was wrong on one detail, and something I wanted to call him out on, just to see his reaction in this new approach. I was already the perfect combination, the one he wanted to be, but I couldn't fire that back at him, not without Clay and the others hearing. I stayed silent, but that appeared to frustrate him, and his iron grip pulled me in closer.

"Why fight it? It's inevitable. Our paths are destined to cross again. They did once, and will again, and there is no reason we have to be adversaries. There is so much for both of us to gain."

He, Clay, pulled me in again, closer, too close. Jean's face disappeared just before it happened. Our lips touched, and Clay's arms firmly pulled me closer. I didn't resist. His touch created a spark that set off a yearning deep inside, and spurred several wanton thoughts that allowed my body to betray my heart. My arms responded by tightening around him before I knew what I was doing. A single hand released its grip. It slowly, lightly, caressed my cheek and traced across my chin. I felt the back of his fingers brushing down my neck, ever so softly before running up and down the chain of my blood charm. I yanked away from him with everything I had.

Standing in front of me was a surprised Clay, as Styx finished the last bars of the song. I collected myself as fast as I could, and said, "Thank you for the nice dance." There was no fake southern accent this time. Just my quivering voice as I tried to construct my exit plan. I needed a few moments alone, and to address the runes immediately and to deal with what had just happened. Seeing all the spying eyes at the other end of the deck gave me that out. I leaned forward and whispered, "I think a few others would like to dance."

With that, Clay and I walked back down to the others where he sat down and was quickly swarmed by Laura and Apryl. Once Mike retrieved Laura, Clay was all Apryl's, and I made my leave. Jennifer asked me if I was okay, and I told her I just needed to take care of something. "You did good," she said.

"Thanks."

16

"Okay, so what is it today? Want me to recite all the symbols again from start to finish?" I hoped that was it. The recent events had me feeling more than a little distracted by immense guilt.

"No," laughed Master Thomas. "You have those memorized quite well, and you show excellent control in their use. But memorization and mastery are two completely different topics."

Mr. Demius nodded his agreement as he stepped down the stairs of his class to the bottom where I stood. "Far different. The question is do you know the difference?"

Well, they were two different words, but that was about it, and that was about as much as I could muster at the moment. If today was going to be full of deep philosophical conversations, I was in trouble.

I knew all the symbols and their meanings by heart. My mother used to make me sit and recite them every day. When I got older, she had me add one more step to the exercise and perform them while I recited them. She said she wanted me to feel them, and not just know them. Only recently did I tell her I finally understood what she meant. Maybe it was something I couldn't sense because I was so young, or maybe it just took years of exposure to them for me to feel the slight differences each symbol created in the energy around me. That made her smile, and she told me that many witches never feel it. They just know them, like memorizing words for a spelling test, or their multiplication tables. The true power came from feeling, is what she said. That had to be what they were talking about. What else could it be? "Feeling the symbols."

"Wrong!" yelled Master Thomas as he hopped up on the table in the front row. An act that drew a scowl from Mr. Demius. My balloon full of pride began losing some air.

"Well, not entirely wrong," corrected Mr. Demius, putting a little air back in my balloon. "No one can master any type of magic without feeling it. Those that don't feel, just perform. But that is just the first step to mastering magic, and the path to mastery has many steps."

"All right, what's the next step." I looked back and forth between my two mentors.

"I'm afraid my dark friend there might have misled you a bit," Master Thomas said from high atop his perch. "There is no map for those steps, and everyone's path from this point is different. Think of feeling the magic. The difference in each symbol. This is only the beginning. From here you must become familiar with it. Know it, like you do your own," Master Thomas choked off his speech and gave me a wry smile. "I almost said your own breathing. Which," a finger pointed up as he hopped down to join us on the floor, "you should take as a compliment. You appear just like any other witch to me, but as I was saying, you need to feel the magic, not think it. Not have to think about what you want to do, but feel what you want to happen and just let it happen. It may sound corny to say, but become one with it. Mother nature doesn't think about how to make the wind blow, it just blows. That is mastery. Right now, you still think through everything you do. A dozen or more thoughts go through your mind to make sure everything is just perfect. It needs to be second nature."

If only it were just a dozen or more thoughts, and now there was a new one. I needed to be faster. Mr. Helms felt my speed would give me an advantage, but now I was hearing I wasn't fast enough. "Let me guess. More practice will help my speed."

Their laughter let the remaining confidence out of my balloon.

"Larissa, it's not about speed. You are plenty fast enough. Faster than any witch I know." Mr. Demius looked at Master Thomas who agreed with a rather confident nod. "What we speak of is hard to describe, but when you reach it, you will know. Magic won't be something you think about when you perform it. It will be something that is always there, and your understanding of what it is, and the infinite possibilities of what you can do with it, will grow beyond your wildest dreams. Then you will become what we all used to be. A true witch. There are just a handful or so of us left. You are correct. Practice is how you will achieve this."

Master Thomas walked over to me, a concerned look on his face. "Demius, I think we are missing something here." He stood in front of me and lightly gripped both of my shoulders.

"What?" I asked, echoing the concern I saw in his face.

"We haven't asked you if you want to. We have just assumed you agreed to everything." He let go of my shoulders and looked down at the floor as he turned away from me. There was another statement hanging there ready to be said. I could sense it in his body language, and he was hesitant to say it. Even Mr. Demius could see it. That much was obvious in how he leaned forward anxiously and watched Master Thomas as he walked around the room. "And I would be remiss if I didn't admit that I hoped you would continue teaching it to others to keep it alive and part of our culture."

"Is this part forbidden too?" I asked thinking of the symbols, which were regarded as old magic and a crime against someone's law to teach anymore.

"Not specifically, just not taught," interjected Mr. Demius.

"Why not?" I asked, but it didn't take me long, half a breath by the others, before the answer hit me. "Power. Just like the symbols."

"Bingo," clapped Master Thomas. "I told you she was a smart one. If you hold people back from reaching their maximum potential who can challenge you?"

I felt I had just found myself in the middle of one of those political thrillers Mr. Bolden liked to read. Someone in power, most likely corrupt, and the struggle of the main character to overcome every obstacle to take their rightful place restoring peace to the world. While those characters may have conveniently not really wanted to be in power, reluctant heroes were a big part of thriller movies and books that appeared targeted at men, and they were also a theme I picked up on when I read Plato's "Republic", there was one major difference between me and them. I wasn't just reluctant. I wanted nothing to do with it. Now I just needed to tell them, but how?

"It is more than that. We are losing who we are as a people. Only a select few are allowed to learn this, which is wrong. We should teach all witches in this way," Mr. Demius stated, showing a level of passion I hadn't seen from the normally dark and very demure member of the faculty here. "I couldn't care less about the council and what happens at those levels, but I do care who we are as a people. We are just shadows of what we used to be, and that needs to be corrected. If you will permit us to teach you, you will be able to teach future generations, help to correct this wrong, and restore us to who we are, much as we are helping to teach you to return you to who your mother intended for you to become."

They did not sell me with their latest plea until that last sentence, and even then, they weren't trying to sell me on anything. This was an all out, world class guilt trip, and that made it even more uncomfortable to turn down than if they were asking me to join some grand fight for control of the council, which I didn't want anything to do with either. This almost seemed noble. Could I refuse it with all everyone was doing for me? Was it really too much to ask? I was looking for a way to pay it back, and I had started that process in the vampire world, was this my way to do the same for my other half? "I accept." The proclamation was made with no specific question asking for my agreement, but they met it with a joint enthusiasm.

"Wonderful." Master Thomas sprung around; his normal hyper personality returned. "It's going to be a lot of work, but I have no doubt that you will be able to handle it."

"Okay," I said even though I was still partially unclear what IT was. IT was something that would take a lot of work, and something I would know when I finally achieved IT. IT sounded a little fishy to me, but I trusted the two men who were standing there smiling back at me, and they had faith in me, that I hoped wasn't misplaced. Not to mention, who was I to turn down a chance to achieve mastery of my abilities as a witch. It sounded like it would get me past the control and a few of the challenges I still struggled with. Where was the downside?

Of course, I was the person who over-thought everything, and what does over-thinking lead to? Doubts. And there was a big doubt percolating in my head that was as terrifying as it was disappointing. What if I couldn't do what they asked? Not for lack of effort, but for lack of ability. There was something Mrs. Saxon told me about on my first day here, and then I asked Mrs. Tenderschott about it after I witnessed it myself. Now that I had my memories back, I knew it hadn't happened for me yet. The question is, could it? I had passed the event's normal time.

"Larissa, we will help you as much as we can through every step of the way. There is no reason to dismay," Master Thomas promised. He was looking at me, bobbing his head back and forth, while looking at me with concerning eyes.

"I know."

"Then what is it? You seem concerned."

I was, I just wasn't aware I was wearing it on my face. "It's just one thing. What if I can't?"

"You have shown a great ability," Master Thomas responded.

"I haven't ascended yet."

Both men exchanged a quizzical look before they looked back at me.

17

I debated whether to head out to the clearing after they dismissed me from what Apryl and a few of the others had started calling "witchy detention" last night after hearing that I was even going to class on a Sunday. My mind, as usual, had more than a few things rolling around in it, and I was unsure what would be worse, being stuck alone with those thoughts or out in the field playing dodge ball with friends who might still be steamed over my and Clay's rather salacious encounter. I hadn't talked to any of them since it happened, retreating quickly downstairs to tend to the runes, and then passing the rest of the night reading and watching a television that appeared when I needed it to. I was beyond questioning how the connection and channels appeared.

My body answered the question before my mind had a chance to complete the debate, and I walked past the stairs and out into the woods. It was a perfectly overcast day, with a cool nip in the air. Refreshing was the best way to describe it. The perfect level of glow slipped through the clouds producing light shadows on the ground while letting you see the colors of the fall foliage without the harsh sun washing them out with glare.

I knew the clearing Mike referenced. It was one I had run across a few times during a hunt or on one of my walks out to the Cove, which had been lonely since Mrs. Saxon had grounded Nathan for our travels. If I didn't, it wouldn't have been hard to find it. The sounds of loud thuds, smacks, and the whizzing of a ball cutting through the air filled the woods. I sure hoped Rob and Martin knew what they were getting into. They were going to be two bruised werewolves at the end of this.

Each sound became louder as I approached the clearing. A ball obviously missed its target and hit a large, majestic pine, sending reverberations up the trunk and causing the top to whip back and forth wildly. A shower of brown needles rained down on the surrounding area, which included me. A quick run of my fingers through my hair dislodged any that became tangled in my red locks. Yells and jeers echoed through the trees. The sound of fun. The sound of a distraction. That was what ended the debate and I ran toward the clearing to join in.

I stopped, not in the clearing, but a few hundred yards short of it to avoid being smacked by the rogue ball that impacted the ground in front me, creating a gouge like a meteor impact. It shot up a spray of dirt, grass, and leaves covering me. A few spits cleared the gritty debris from my mouth, but that didn't help the rest of me. I was a mess. Dirt and leaves covered every inch of my white sweater and black jeans. There was no doubt there were small pieces of debris and dirt smudge on my face. I blinked a few times to check, and yep, there was a small bit of something in my lashes obscuring my vision. I made a quick blow up, tossing my bangs away from my face and removing whatever was in my eyelashes. Someone just ahead of me at the edge of the clearing stood and watched me wearily.

"Larissa... sorry..." Brad said sounding rather defensive.

I did my best to brush myself off with my hands before I reverted to other means. Once I was done, I was shower fresh standing there with a ball, the ball, at my feet. I held my hand over it, and it rose up out of the impact crater to my hand.

"Larissa... it was an accident..." Brad said in an attempt to apologize.

"Oh, boy..." Martin said when he joined Brad.

Their next reaction I believe was caused by the smirk I had, and the fact I drew the ball back.

"Run!" exclaimed Martin. Brad was already gone, headed back to the clearing. Martin didn't wait to see the ball to leave my hand before he followed. It would appear werewolves are as fast as vampires.

The ball left my hand with a boom, and there was no soft whiz through the air. It thundered, and I followed behind it. I wanted to see it when it hit. When I reached the clearing, I slid to a stop, and watched the ball not disappoint. It whacked Brad first, caroming off his shoulder to hit Martin. It sent both tumbling to the ground and I gave a little fist pump.

"I'm okay," Martin called as he pushed himself up off the floor. "Not that anyone cares," he remarked, and I pouted along with him. Brad was stilling lying on the ground, but he was laughing, which was a good sign.

"We want her. We need all the help we can get," Apryl called from across the clearing. Her team appeared to be Rob, Laura, Mike, and Mr. Bolden—who scoffed at Apryl's assessment of the team's ability.

I was ready to join their effort right up until I locked eyes with a member of the other side who emerged from the woods retrieving a ball. Any enthusiasm I felt before about getting involved blew away on the cool breeze that moved through the clearing. I just couldn't do it. Thoughts, and something else swirled along with the wind. "Not right now. I am just taking a walk."

"Oh, come on. We need the help. Please," Apryl pleaded.

"It was a bad day in witch-detention. I need to clear my head." I said, but my eyes never left Clay's, no matter how much I wanted them to, or how much I needed them to. I headed through the clearing toward the cove with the sounds of Apryl and Mike's objections behind me, even though Mike made a valiant point, "what better way to get over some witch frustration than to pelt some werewolves."

I left feeling the aftereffects of that uncomfortable lock between Clay and my eyes. Those feelings were not alone. So much came flooding over the dam gates of avoidance that I had constructed to keep from obsessing about what had happened. That brief look caused those gates to splinter, letting it all rush through with an unfathomable weight. I expected the worst of it to be guilt related, and it was, but not for the reason I expected. Nathan would be beyond hurt if he ever found out, and I didn't want him to ever feel that way. I absolutely didn't want to be the cause. That I couldn't deal with. If only that were the biggest concern I had at the moment. My guilt was not wholly that. I felt guilty for what I felt, how my body reacted, how everything happened around me at that moment, going all the way back to the first time we touched briefly. That spark. Where the hell did that come from? And why did it happen? Or, the better question, why did I let myself feel that way? I had Nathan. He should be the only person who could stir me, and that was definitely a stirring, like that.

What made it worse, Nathan never made me feel like that. Oh, he stirred me. Nathan stirred me in ways I wasn't about to admit to him. Not now. Not ever. There were simple looks he gave me that took all I had to resist just grabbing him and kissing him. A lot of those times I lost the battle, which I considered wins. When I told him I remembered who I was, I leapt on him on my bed. That moment, the way he smiled up at me. My own hands started reaching for my shirt to shed my clothes and give myself to him, truly and freely. It took every ounce of self-control to hold back. I was unsure if I could trust myself with those passions flowing. There was a burning, but of a different type then.

When Clay touched me, things stirred in a way that was different than Nathan. Everything in the universe lined up, the angels sang and rejoiced, and my skin yearned to feel his against mine. It was more primal, not a giving of myself the way it is with Nathan. I wanted, I needed Nathan to know he had my heart and my soul. With Clay, I just wanted him to have my flesh.

My hands rubbed my temples as those thoughts fought each other as I stood and watched the beautiful water crash against the craggy rock outcroppings. One thought the waves, the other the rocks. Neither wanting to give. I knew which one I wanted to win. Make that which thought had to win. My struggle? Could it win with the other one looming?

"Hey."

I jumped. Both from the sound of a voice disturbing the tranquility of this spot which I wanted to replicate inside, but also from the sound of the southern drawl that delivered it. The way that one syllable word became two, both from his accent and an emotion. A level of comfort that I didn't want him to feel around me.

"Clay, I want to be alone," I stated without turning around.

"I know, but I think we need to talk."

"You don't understand the concept of being alone, do you?" I turned off my filter allowing the full weight of my annoyance to resonate in my words.

"Actually, I do. I know the concept and feeling very well. I was alone until Mr. Bolden found me..."

He obviously didn't get it, so I stopped it before this went any further. "No, you don't. Look," I started to turn around but didn't. I didn't trust myself to say what I needed to if I was looking at him, and that made me feel sick. "Clay, what happened shouldn't have happened. I don't know why it did—I had my suspicion—but that doesn't matter. It shouldn't have, and it can't happen again. That is all I have to say about it."

"That is it?"

"Yes, that is it." This time I made it a statement removing any emotion from the words. No annoyance, but strong like the rocks.

"You can't say you didn't feel it."

"I didn't," I lied. "All I felt was a something we shouldn't be doing."

"There is no way you didn't. I felt your body react." His voice was now closer. Just behind me. "Your arms wrapped around me and held on."

"I felt I was about to fall." Oh lord, what a lame excuse, and Clay knew it. There was a giggle behind me. Why did he giggle? Oh crap, it came off as flirtatious. Why did I say that?

"I will always be there to catch you," he remarked, and his hand reached and firmly touched the small of my back. Damn, even through my sweater and shirt I felt it. Like an electricity that flowed through me. Paralyzingly strong, and more than a little addicting. Like with any habit, the longer it continued the stronger it became, and this was teetering on the edge. I stepped forward, breaking the connection. My body recoiled and protested against my decision. The nothingness I felt longed to feel that spark again, while both my mind and heart repeated Nathan's name over and over.

"Clay, you need to stop."

"Why? And don't say it is because you are with Nathan."

"That is exactly why." This time I turned around. It was time to face him and end this before things continued too far, not that they hadn't already. We had gone way over the line, and now it was time to walk it back. Chalk it up to a mistake. A brief lapse that his current state of strong emotions and my Jean compromised state contributed too, not that I would tell him about Jean's visit. I made sure to look him right in the eyes and pulled myself together to be as forceful as the crashing waves behind me, hoping to wash this issue with Clay away. "Look, I love Nathan. He is the one for me." It came out as weak as a field mouse.

"No, he's not," Clay remarked.

"Oh, he is. Absolutely. Not a question about it," I insisted.

"Let me ask you this? Has he ever made you feel like that before?" Clay paced in a circle. "And before you answer," he held his finger up, "I have got to say, nothing, nothing has ever made me feel like that before. Even sex. I know how stupid it sounds, but it does. Just touching you felt better than my first time or any time since, and I think I know why."

I didn't ask. I didn't want to know that there was some logic behind this. I didn't care. Well, that wasn't exactly true. My heart didn't care, and neither did my mind. My body wanted some more. I didn't know if he was right though. I haven't even been with anyone before, but I could confirm it was a feeling unlike anything I had felt before, even from Nathan, and I wasn't going to admit that to Clay.

"I will tell you why. It is because we are both vampires. It is our DNA, or something like that. Everything in us is amped up a hundred times more than normal. Which I believe includes our effect on each other."

With that he grabbed me again, and I struggled to break free, but only for a moment. That intoxicating feeling forced my body to surrender, present the first argument and closing on the case on Clay's theory. He was right. He had to be. Why else would I be melting like this for him?

Inside I heard myself screaming no, but my body wasn't taking the call. It was giving a busy signal as it was completely focused on what his hand was doing in the center of my back. His touch light, firm and controlling. All I could do was watch as my own body betrayed my heart. I felt destroyed as he leaned in. His lips touched mine, and that was all it took. Any chance of resistance gone, and just like how Clay described that night at the Christmas tree party, I was along for the ride, with someone else controlling the wheel.

He pulled back, just inches away and whispered, "This is why we need to be together. Vampires and vampires." His hand slid down my arm, and in the split second when he grabbed for my hand, reality snapped back, and I slapped him across the face, and put something extra behind it sending him flying back into the woods.

18

I left Clay out there in the woods to find his own way back. He seemed like a big boy. I was sure he could handle it. What I needed was to be as far away from him as possible, but that didn't mean heading right back to the coven. Though in the end I did. No amount of thought erased what I felt. If anything, it made it worse. Clay was right. He had to be. That was the only explanation for what I felt, how I reacted, and how he reacted when we were together. The why made sense too. It was a fact I couldn't dismiss. Logic would not be a help here. What I needed was something that would touch me on a different level, and seeing the sun going down meant it wouldn't be long, and this time I would be there waiting on them.

That was right where I was when Amy and Nathan appeared for our nightly time together. I was sitting there in the chair waiting. Amy's eyes burst wide open, and she ran to hug me, and Nathan gave me a surprised look. He was always the one who was rather punctual. Now it was my turn. I greeted him with a hug and a kiss which either how fast I moved in for it or how long it lasted took his breath away. That didn't stop me from going in for a second one. This one shorter, and it was for me, not him. I let him go and felt flat. There was still the spark, our spark, but compared to what I felt with Clay, this was just a fizzle. I hid my disappointment as we settled down with Amy in my lap with book in hand, wasting no time to dive right into the story and try to put that behind me.

That worked until I watched Amy walk in through the door with Ms. Parrish. Then I was there, face to face with reality, unable to shake the thought that maybe he was right, but also unable to shake the fact that I was more than a vampire, and there was more to a relationship than a physical yearning, but oh that yearning. It was hard to forget. My solution avoidance, and trying to go on with normal life, even though mine was anything but and I still had a rather frightening prospect to deal with tonight.

"I thought it had to be at midnight on your 18th birthday?"

"So did I," I said, assuming both Nathan and I were told by the same person, his mother. "Master Thomas said it has to be at least after your 18th birthday. Actually, performing it on that day was more of a ritual that has held through time. Kind of a formality to give young witches something to look forward to. He compared it to a second Christmas."

"Well, you are definitely after…"

I shot a look at Nathan freezing him mid-sentence. My age had become something of a joke between us, and each reaction was playful. It even was again this time, but there was a serious concern around it. "Yes and no. By the calendar I am, but in other ways I never reached that age."

The surprised look on Nathan's face was the very same one I saw on Master Thomas' when I made the same point. My uniqueness again was a complication, and one no one knew the answer for.

"Will it still work?" asked Nathan.

The only answer I could give him was the same conclusion both Mr. Demius and Master Thomas reached, even after consulting a few others while I was going through their exhausting exercises. "There is only one way to find out. We are doing it tonight at midnight."

I was concerned. Well, that might not be a strong enough word for it. My only experience with this was less than pleasant, and I was only an observer then. This time it was all about me, and no one could tell me what to expect. Which was the same for everyone. The results and experience were individual, but I had just a few extenuating factors that made this a little more unpredictable, and more than a little uncomfortable. That was why I peered across the table at Nathan and made a request that I already knew the answer to. "Come with me?"

Nathan was a little surprised by the question and quickly shook it off. "You know the rules. I can walk you as far as the door, but that is it. I can't come in, but I can tell you what I can do though." His hand reached across the table, and I met it halfway. His fingers intertwined with mine making a perfect union between us. I felt our connection. It was strong. That couldn't be disputed. It was deep, and at this moment, the lack of that spark that set me on fire seemed unimportant. "I will wait right outside and be there for you when it is all over with."

Why I felt disappointed, I didn't know. There wasn't a chance in hell he was going to be allowed to come in with me. I knew that before I even asked, and it wouldn't do any good to talk to Mrs. Saxon either about bending the rules this one time. They made the sanctity of this ritual very clear to me, in a way that made me believe that an outsider might interfere. All I could accept was Nathan's counteroffer, but I needed to clarify a detail first. "Right outside the door? The whole time?"

"Right outside the door. I won't go anywhere," he promised.

"All right," I agreed. It would have to do. What other option did I have? I let go of his hand and collapsed back in my chair. My head felt drained from the work Master Thomas and Mr. Demius put me through, and my emotions were on edge from ... everything.

"Try to relax. I do have some good news to share."

"What is that?" I feigned curiosity. There was too much going on around me at the moment and I never really wanted to appear to be a self-absorbed person. That was the opposite of who I was, or who I thought and hoped I was. At the moment though, I just didn't have the capacity to look beyond myself. My give-a-crap tank was full, and unfortunately it was all my crap.

"My mom is letting me out of house arrest," he said with a wide smile. "She said we have behaved ourselves."

"That's great." My response didn't sound as enthusiastic as it should have to that news. An effect of the weight of everything else holding it back. I had to correct it, so I added, "It really is. I have missed our walks." I put the best coy look I could produce at the moment on my face. The look on Nathan's face told me it wasn't that convincing.

"Relax. Tonight is going to be just fine."

"I know." I didn't, but that is just what you say when someone tells you everything is going to be fine. It was the polite thing to do. Screaming the truth wasn't going to change anything. It would not make me feel any less scared. It wasn't going to answer any of the questions I had. What would, even temporarily, was a distraction. "We have an English quiz tomorrow. Probably need to get some studying done."

The topic, Shakespearean Sonnets, which I have read more times than I could remember, while, Nathan from the sounds of it, had only scanned them. I seriously doubted his mother would make us quote them, which I could. She was probably more into the meaning and the structure, which I was making some progress in conveying to Nathan, even though he was complaining his head was about to explode. It seemed he really enjoyed last year's focus on the modern masters but was struggling with European literature. There was just so much of it, and we covered a little of everything, which from what I had learned of Nathan was the problem. He liked the ability to latch hold of something and focus on it, like he did with me.

"Nice evening for a walk," I looked up and saw Clay, and what light in my mood that may have been restored by this time with Nathan was now gone. I turned away and looked at Nathan. I didn't want to see Clay. Having him out here now went against my plan of avoidance, and my mind had started constructing an excuse for Nathan and myself to head back in. I should have worked faster on that excuse. Nathan slid his chair back a bit. There was a leeriness in his eyes and body language. Based on his first exposure to Clay, I couldn't blame him. I put up a single hand in Nathan's direction, and he stopped, but the fluttering I felt exposed how uncomfortable he was. Unfortunately, the rest of us knew it too.

Apryl, Clay's escort on what I guessed was a moonlit stroll through the woods, rushed to put herself on Clay's side, right between him and Nathan. I tried to make the moment as normal as it should be "It is. Where are you two heading?" My attempt to be coy didn't completely mask the tension of the moment. Clay was burning a hole through me with his glare. His arm wrapped around Apryl's waist before giving her a little squeeze.

"Just a quick walk through the woods before the boys come out to do their sweep," Apryl said with a wink in my direction. I knew exactly what this was. A chance to get Clay alone without Laura hanging around. That was her intention. I wasn't sure Clay was in agreement.

"Well, you two have fun."

"We will. See you later." Apryl was all smiles as she led Clay toward the woods.

In hindsight I should have let them go. I had dodged one of the most uncomfortable moments of recent memory, make that almost. "Hey Apryl. I will be late getting up to the deck tonight. I have a witch thing to do tonight."

She turned and looked back at me curiously. "A witch thing?"

"I will explain as much as I can later." Flashbacks of my hours of being the traitor played in my head. Here we go again. I could almost see it in her face already, and I knew her mind was searching through everyone's birthday to try to figure out who was the lucky one this time. That was my biggest worry, and it was the wrong one.

I said nothing while her mind ran through the possibilities, but Clay did, and his words cut deeper than the sharpest knife. "Don't be too long. I would like another dance, Miss Dubois."

I had to get over the shock, surprise, and hurt in a split second to catch Nathan who was out of his chair surprisingly fast. "Dance?" he asked, sounding rather controlled while his eyes were narrowing into something less attractive.

"It was nothing. He danced with everyone," I tried to explain, and Apryl attempted to rush Clay out to the woods for their walk alone, but he had stopped dead in his tracks.

"Hey new kid!" I reached for Nathan. Hoping to calm him down without having to use anything on him. "Stay away from my girlfriend!"

Inside I was pleading for Clay to just keep walking. There was no reason for him to do anything else. No reason for him to bring up what happened after the dance, or earlier today. Apryl was urging him to do the same, but for her own selfish reasons and I was all for those. Instead, Clay stepped back on the pool deck. Nathan pushed his chair aside and came around the table in some sort of show of immature machismo. He should know better, especially after what he witnessed last night.

"Nathan, let it go." I warned. "You too Clay." I wanted to make sure both knew they were in the wrong, but other things were at play here. Nathan had his teenage hormones, which were bad, but they were no match for what was roaring through Clay, and I could tell we were just seconds before this was going to be out of hand, if it already wasn't.

Both took another step and ran into a brick wall I threw in front of each of them. I could hold them from each other easily, but I shouldn't have to. Clay had an excuse, and in time he would learn how to control it. Or should I say, I hoped he will learn how to control it, just as I hoped with all my will he wouldn't say anything else. I even considered influencing him in the matter, and may have passed a simple suggestion to him for my own safety.

Nathan, on the other hand, had a lot of growing up to do and needed to show some trust in me. That was what bothered me the most. Though I had some significant doubts if I really deserved it. I felt that pang, and as horrible as it was for me to feel, it didn't even come close to what Nathan would do if he knew.

Clay made another shove against the immovable blockade I put in front of him, and then gave in to Apryl's yank on his arm. The two went walking out to the woods. Clay only looked back once. Apryl did twice, both times she mouthed "Sorry."

Nathan stood right where I had blocked him, and if he had been a cartoon character, steam would have been shooting from his ears. This was the third time since Clay arrived that his jealous bone had reached up and bit him. That wasn't an attractive look in my book. It was a book I slammed shut, along with the literature book and notebooks and stormed past him.

"Maybe I'm not the one who needs to ascend!" I roared from the path leading inside.

19

To say Nathan and I had it out after we walked inside would be like saying Mount Vesuvius only burped. My anger and disappointment grew with every step toward the door. His lack of trust was a big thing for me. I wasn't sure why. It wasn't like I had a series of bad relationships in my past. But, maybe that was it. I didn't have any relationships in my past. Not a one. It didn't matter. He was wrong, and I wanted to make sure that was perfectly clear. Though I was ignoring the elephant sized hypocrisy in the room.

After I did so, I wondered if I had made it too clear. There was no one to walk me to the ascension, and no one to wait for me after. Not his choice. It was all mine. He even pushed the point saying he was still going to be there, but I kept rejecting him. Something I didn't plan to do often, but it was effective. I lost track of how many times he apologized and agreed with me. I even felt some of the apologies were genuine and he actually agreed he had no reason to be jealous of Clay or anyone else, ever. The puppy dog eyes were a nice touch. He even tried to hug me, and instead of just pulling away like I had the other times we had fought, I put up a block again and stood on the other side with my arms crossed. That might have been when I crossed the line. More so than the yelling, which caused a few heads to pop out of the doors. Each received a look from me that sent them back. When I thought back on it, it would seem I had channeled my own version of the wicked witch, and if not that bad, at least a good impersonation of a Gwen-fit.

The walk down to the ritual room was a lonely journey. Normally in these moments my mind would be running away with itself over any number of questions. If I had to guess this time it would be pondering all the possibilities of what would happen at my ascension, but it wasn't. The only thoughts that existed were how lonely the walk was and how much of a mess the one happy spot in my life was. Lisa had walked in with the others, and here I was approaching the door alone. When I entered it seemed like I was even more alone, except maybe for those stupid cherubs up above. I regarded them with a whispered warning, "It hasn't been a good night, so don't push me."

A familiar giggle came from behind the curtain. When it parted, I saw Mrs. Tenderschott walking through, wearing a black hooded gown just like she had for Lisa's ceremony. Just like that time, she carried an extra one for me and handed it to me. I quickly donned it. "Those little things do look evil don't they?" she asked looking up.

"One day I am going to set them a blaze." I swear I heard them give a quick laugh of protest at that remark.

"I am so happy you are going through this," started a cheery Mrs. Tenderschott, but her mood didn't last long. "I'm not sure how this is going to go, but I am happy nonetheless."

She reached around and helped straighten the hood before she pulled it up over my head. I had concerns before, and a little bit of fear, but feeling the darkness of the hood envelop me set things on fire, and I felt a single tear form in the corner of my eye.

"They covered what to say, correct?"

"Yes," I replied, still surprised at how simple it was. When I watched before, I felt it was some odd phrase in a different language, but it wasn't. Just an odd combination of words that produced a rhythm. "Family of my life, life of my family"

"Good. All you have to do is sit there and say that low and monotone. Let the room and the ceremony do the rest."

I wanted to ask several questions. How will I know if the answer was yes? Will it hurt? What if it is a no? Would I feel anything at all? Was it dangerous to even try this? And many more, but I didn't. I didn't need to. I already knew the answer, or answers, that I would receive to each and every one of them. It is different for everyone, and they had no idea because there was no one like me.

I felt my right hand tremble a little against my side, so I reached over with the left and held it, hoping to reassure it, but that was useless as my left hand was trembling even harder than its partner. A cold breeze sent a shiver through me, and we hadn't even started yet, but a look back at the curtain told me we had. Gwen came through leading the others. All dressed in black, just like before. Her reception was as cold as ever, and I felt Mrs. Tenderschott's hand nudge me toward my position in the center of the room. A place I had stood many times before, and none of them were good.

I took my place, inside the circle of runes that I now recognized what they said and meant. My fellow witches surrounded around me. All smiling, well all except one. Gwen wasn't frowning either. She had a stern look on her face, and her eyes were locked on me. Lisa looked at me from under her hood and mouthed, "Relax and go with it."

I nodded.

The instructors and a few distinguished guests entered next. I thought Gwen's eyes were going to pop out of her head when Master Thomas entered. She wasn't the only one. Marcia gasped. Along with him were Mr. Nevers and Mrs. Mauro, two of what I had heard were members of the growing fan club I had among the council. Of course, only Mr. Nevers knew what I was being tutored in.

The chant started with the teachers. The students joined in after the first word. I was in by the third. "Family of my life. Life of my Family. Family of my life. Life of my Family. Family of my life. Life of my Family. Family of my life. Life of my Family."

There was no burst of moonlight through the glass above to illuminate me as the star of some freaky dark witchcraft show, like had happened for Lisa. At least not that I noticed. I could be the center of nature's spotlight, and I wouldn't know it. All I saw in my eyes were the images of my mother, my father, my grandparents, and people I had to assume were earlier generations of my family. All smiling as they moved past me. Even the Nortons, which didn't make any sense to me; they weren't witches.

A light tap on my shoulder startled me, and I jumped around into a crowd of people, as they walked past me. I recognized their faces; I had just seen them moments ago flashing before my eyes. Now they were walking past me, regarding me as they did. They formed a circle around me, just like the witches in the coven had. Unlike them, they stood silently. I felt weepy as my father passed by. I reached out for his hand. His touch so kind and warm, as were his brown eyes. He didn't stop. How I wanted him to. I wanted to give him a hug. Behind him was the last one, my own mother. She looked like I had seen her in my many trips back to see her. She wore a black pencil dress as she came to a stop right in front of me. I stood there, fighting back the tears, as she reached forward and grabbed my hands. She looked at me with both pride and confusion.

"Hi Mom," my voice squeaked through the flood of emotions that threatened to drown me. It no longer sounded like the younger version of me. The me, she remembered and held dear. It was now the real me.

"Larissa," she said, fighting against her own tears. "This is one the proudest moments for a mother. The moment her daughter comes into her own. I am surprised it is happening today. This is not your birthday, and trust me a mother knows her child's birthday." She let out a nervous laugh and paused as if she wanted for me to explain. I couldn't. Not here, and not now. "You have always been on the path to be an excellent addition to our community, but you must remember. This is not the end of your journey. This is your beginning. You must continue to learn and perfect your craft, but most importantly you must give back by teaching the next generation. Pass on your knowledge and skill. That is the only way we continue. We don't live forever. Will you promise to do that?"

"I will," I replied.

"Of course, you will. You are my daughter after all. Now go forth and make us proud."

With that, she was gone, as was everyone else around us except my circle of peers and instructors who continued to chant. I looked up for the moonbeam like what Lisa had, but there was nothing coming through the skylight. Instead, a storm brewed above with flashes of distant lightning outlining the rolling clouds. One bolt wasn't so distant, and it shocked me to see it crash through the skylight striking me while the ground rolled and heaved under my feet. I attempted to jump out of the way, but not even a vampire could beat a lightning strike. It didn't hurt. My body vibrated from my feet to the tip of my head, and I heard the loud clap. The longer the vibration lasted the weaker my body felt. I tried to steady myself as much as possible, but eventually my knees gave. I looked out to see if anyone was coming to help me, but it was only then that I noticed the world was moving in slow motion around me. Sparks and shards of glass showered down, but hadn't reached the ground. A few of the others had started to shield themselves from the coming shower.

I hit the floor around the same time as the sparks did. The glass shards still had several feet to go to reach the dark wooden floor. I was flat on the floor when time returned to normal, and I heard the crashing of the glass. Below me the floor continued to roll and tilt, or I thought it did. It could have been me. The chanting stopped and the others filed out, leaving me there on the floor. I wanted to push up and follow them, but that feeling of the world moving all around me was still there, and it was growing by the second. When I pushed up to my knees I had a moment of wooziness, and the room made a quick spin. I was about to blame the cherubs above, but I had a feeling what it was, but I didn't know why it was.

My first step up was an exploratory move. When I didn't fall, I went ahead and stood up the rest of the way. Mrs. Tenderschott emerged from the shadows. She moved cautiously through the broken glass to the center of the circle. "Are you all right?" She pulled the hood off of my head. "You are all wide-eyed and... well... wired looking."

"I think so," I responded timidly, just like how my body was responding to what it felt. She said it better than I could have. That was exactly how I felt, wired. My body still vibrated all over from the lightning strike, and simple things like standing there took an effort to steady myself. The air, and everything around me felt strangely different. It felt like something, instead of the nothingness of normal air.

"It will wear off." She helped to pull the black hooded gown over my head. Every muscle in my body worked to steady myself as the fabric tugged me from one side to the other.

"Does everyone feel like this?" I asked, feeling rather uninformed and even more unprepared for this than I did before it happened. Mrs. Saxon explained what the premise was a while ago, and earlier today Master Thomas took his shot, which wasn't as eloquent. I had asked both of them about the process; how it worked. They both gave me the same answer, it's different for everyone. To me that sounded like a convenient answer, and a little bit of a cop out.

"Everyone feels different after. That is, if the answer was yes," replied Mrs. Tenderschott, now folding my black gown.

"It's like the entire world..."

"Shhh," she shushed me quickly. "Larissa, the experience is personal to you, and you shouldn't share it."

"Oh," I gasped and jumped at the abrupt interruption, almost losing my balance.

As her hand reached up to my shoulder and gently rubbed it, her grandmotherly look had returned. "I am sorry. I didn't mean for that to sound so harsh, but it is important for you to learn, that is something you can never share with anyone."

"Is it a secret or something?" That was a question I had to ask for my own curiosity, but one thing that had stuck with me was the promise I made my mother. It was strangely similar to the request Master Thomas and Mr. Demius had asked me as well. And for some reason, right now, all of that seemed to blend together and overpowered any thoughts of myself and what I had just gone through. There was a feeling of responsibility, my responsibility. I needed to know why.

"Yes and no," she said with a quirky smile. She wrapped an arm around my shoulder and helped me walk toward the door. "Someone's ascension is a very personal experience. It has to be that way. Everyone is different. Different families, different experiences, and different capabilities. It is meant to be a life altering event, both in the person's capability and their maturity. Now you could tell me what you experienced and how you feel, and it won't cause any problems. I have already ascended and so have you. My knowing what you went through won't take away any of the weight and impact of what I felt, and it would be the same if I told you what I went through, but if you tell Gwen who goes through it next month, well... what she experienced may be different from what you did. That may take away from the impact of the moment on her, and change how it shapes her. This is why you can never speak of it, just in case someone else hears that shouldn't." She stopped us short of the curtain and pushed it aside and looked around to make sure no one was hiding behind it, and then smiled like a mischievous child. "Now if you want, you can tell me."

I stood there for a few moments and told her what I saw during it. Even with the warning she had just given me, I needed to talk to someone about it, and it wasn't to share what I felt, but to share the request that my mother had made of me. Upon hearing it, Mrs. Tenderschott nodded in agreement.

"I am not surprised she made that request. Remember who she was in our community."

I nodded, still feeling the vibration, but it had moved to more of a background sensation, now behind the world around me instead of on the surface.

"It is a great responsibility, and one I know you will excel at. In some ways, all of us have that role, but most never do it." She pulled me in for a warm grandmotherly hug. "I am so proud of you. Your mother would be too. That I have no doubt of." For the second time tonight, a tear threatened to escape from the corners of my eyes.

"You feeling better?" she pushed me back at arm's length. I nodded because I was. My hands no longer felt like they were shaking, and the volume of the vibration had been turned down yet another notch. We walked together out the door. Outside another form of comfort waited for me. Even though I told him not to, he was there. It would seem my rebellious streak had spread to him.

20

I wouldn't say Nathan was forgiven by being there afterwards. The problem that caused our minor blow up just didn't seem to be that important anymore in the grand scheme of things. Something of a trivial immature blow up of emotions that I was sure would happen several more times, and one day I might find the shoe on the other foot. A thought that made me shudder, but not one I could dismiss as a possibility.

We didn't speak of it, and we didn't speak of my ascension beyond a single question. "Are you okay?"

To which I replied, "I am."

That was it. We walked toward the hall and paused a moment to just sit and admire the Christmas tree that was in full glory with a nice dusting of flurries on its branches. A full-sized gingerbread house now stood in the corner where I had thrown Clay last night. Nothing around this place surprised me anymore. Well, maybe some things did. I couldn't help myself and had to lean in to smell the walls, unsure why I even thought to question if it was real or not. Then I grabbed Nathan by the hand and walked inside it where we found gingerbread furniture and a real working fireplace.

"We have to show Amy," I remarked, feeling like a little girl myself as I studied the ornaments that were on the small tree inside. Of course, they were made out of gingerbread. All that was missing was a gingerbread family.

"We will."

I pulled Nathan closer in our little private sanctuary. My arms wrapped around him, and he returned the gesture, and I saw him again staring into my eyes. Something he had mentioned before he loved doing, but I never understood it. They were black and emotionless. Like looking at two shiny black rocks. He needed better. He needed to see two windows into my soul that told him how I was feeling. I felt the tingle just over the vibration that still remained. It started at the top of my head and worked its way down to my feet. I watched for the reaction, and all I saw was a quick eye shift as he took in my rosy cheeks and blue eyes. Then I felt the little squeeze from his arms that told me he liked the feeling of the warmth of my body. A contrast to the normally cold presence.

"Better?" I whispered into his ear, letting my warm breath dance around his ear.

He didn't take long to respond. That meant the response was true, and from the heart, and knowing that meant everything to me when I heard what it was. "It doesn't matter to me either way. You are you, and that is all that matters."

I was touched and moved, and for the third time tears threatened, but again I forced them back, though it was harder this time than the others, and I used sarcasm to cover that effort. "Smooth."

He held me for what felt like forever, but it was nowhere near long enough, and when he tried to release me, I held on tighter, and added some encouragement to keep him engaged. His lips didn't protest, and like always, after I initiated, I let him take over. Feeling the warmth sent a tingle through me, something I hadn't felt before. It still wasn't what I felt with Clay, but I was okay with that. There was so much more to us than that, and that was what mattered. I was hooked, and had to hold back a little to not let things get out of hand between us. Nathan was free to do what he wanted and found no objection as his hands roamed around a little into territory he hadn't ventured before. To think he used to worry that holding hands was too tempting for me.

Afterward we cautiously exited the gingerbread house, not waiting to be caught by anyone, and he walked me up to my door where we said good night. I stood there and watched him walk back down the hall and out of the door. When it closed, I waved my hand, creating a portal that I could peer through. Mr. Demius should be proud. I conjured the all-seeing eye in just a blink.

I watched him walk down the stairs and all the way back to his room in Mrs. Saxon's residence. I should have closed it there, but I didn't. I watched as he kicked off his shoes and lingered in front of the window, looking out at the clear moonlight night. It was a tranquil sight, and one I hoped to replicate shortly up on the deck, and I would have done it sooner if he hadn't peeled off the skintight shirt he wore and tossed it back on his bed. I had seen Nathan without his shirt around the pool many times, and my hands had traced the ripples of every muscle more times than I could remember, and it was a strong memory. My fingers were exploring from where I was while I watched the moonlight dance across his chest.

Nathan yawned and left the window, and I thought he was going to sit down on his bed. Maybe swing his legs up and go to sleep or something, but I had missed one detail that he might need to take care of before that, and what I thought was him bending to sit down was him bending to take off his pants. My brain yelled at me to close the portal, but my hands didn't reply. They were too busy making another pass over his chest and remembering the one time they explored his butt while searching for his cell phone. It was a short pass, and they were wondering what it would take to get a longer and a more meaningful one. I saw a hint of navy-blue boxers as his pants slid down. My eyes went elsewhere when they reached his mid-thigh. It was then when my brain won out and my hands finally reacted and closed the portal, and

I leaned back against the wall by my door. My temporary human form felt flushed and was breathing hard. A second quick wave of my hand returned me back to my normal self, but that didn't stop that image from dancing in my head.

Quickly I walked through my door and up the stairs to the deck, more than slightly embarrassed by my indiscretion. It was probably not the most responsible use of magic, but I doubted I was the first to do it. Then I wondered if Jack ever, but I stopped there. I stepped up on the deck and was mobbed by everyone, including both Jennifer and Kevin Bolden. "You're alive!" screamed Pam, but then she realized what she had said.

"I am okay, and before anyone asks, remember, I can't tell you anything about it." I hoped everyone heeded my warning, and we weren't going to have a repeat of what had happened before.

"We are just happy you are okay." Jennifer stepped forward. I wasn't sure if they elected her as the spokesperson of the group, or she was asserting herself to make sure no one else crossed the line, but what I could tell was there was something on her mind. "Can we ask just one question?" She held her hand up and pinched her fingers together to indicate what she perceived as the size of the question.

"What is it?" I hadn't agreed or declined the request. Which I would end up doing would depend on the question.

"Did it work? Is that okay to ask?"

"That was two questions." I let that simmer with them as I walked to the area where we always sat. I felt their gaze burning a hole in the back of my head. Without turning around, I stopped and stood solemnly, and said, "Yes."

There were several squeals from behind me followed by Pam and Laura draped around my neck. Mike stood uncomfortably and said, "Congratulations?" He looked at the others, "I don't know. Is that something you say in situations like this?"

"Yes," I assured him, which he seemed to appreciate. "Thank you."

Most gave me a pat on the back or delivered their own congratulations as they walked past me.

When Clay approached, I tried to turn and walk the other way. I could sense there was much more on his mind, and this wasn't because I had obtained Jack's talent during ascension. It was written all over his face, and the hesitation in his movements as he approached me, and I wasn't in the mood, especially not here, in front of everyone.

"Congratulations Larissa," he said with his comforting southern drawl. I wanted to keep walking, but I was well aware that it would come off as rude up here in front of the others, and no one knew about what happened out in the cove. I turned around reluctantly, and he stood there fidgeting in the awkward silence. There was something else. It was there, I could tell, and I sure hoped it wasn't what I thought it was. He made a few quick glances over my shoulder and after the last one I turned to see what he was looking at and caught Apryl spinning away from me. My discomfort grew, as did my flight instinct. When I turned back, he looked again, and finally spoke. "I am sincerely sorry for earlier. I was wrong about how I behaved around you and Nathan."

"It's fine Clay. Nothing to worry about." I hoped my curtness in my tone and in how I quickly spun away from him wasn't too harsh.

"And..." he started. There was a longing in his voice that grabbed me like a lasso and pulled me back. When I turned, I saw it also caught Apryl, probably not as its main target, but she was a very interested piece of collateral damage by the look on her face as she looked on to see what he would say next.

"Really Clay, it's fine. Nothing to worry about," I reassured, with a suggested thought ready to go if needed. His hands swung at his side as he looked back at Apryl and then at me. Then an odd cock of his head during his last glance at me before he turned and went to join the others to resume the mean game of Monopoly they had started before I arrived. An interesting choice of game, considering the council's concern about vampires.

"Nice coaching." Apryl played dumb as she sat down next to me at the other end of our area. Music, 80s pop, was playing softly in the background. Jennifer joined me in my focus on Apryl, waiting for a confirmation. She had put Clay up to it, there wasn't any doubt.

It didn't take long before she cracked. "He and I had a long talk while we walked. I think he learned something. You're not the only one who can teach and help people around here."

Jennifer and I exchanged a look, and right on cue, both of us reached over and gave Apryl high-five. "Welcome to the club," I added, full of hope that their long walk included more than just that talk.

"Oh, and you are forgiven." Apryl smugly sat back in her chair. I felt something I shouldn't have been able to. My heart sinking. My vision narrowed, and I dug my fingers into the arms of the chair to steady myself. "The kiss last night." Apryl said with a little giggle. "Larissa, are you okay? You look like you saw a ghost." She leaned over and put her hand on mine, but didn't notice the holes my fingers had clawed into the cushion.

"That wasn't me!" I exclaimed.

"Relax," interrupted Apryl. "I know. Clay told me he lost control after the dance. The emotions on overload and all. I couldn't let the opportunity go to give you a little grief."

"Gee, thanks," I remarked.

Apryl leaned forward against the arm of her chair, and stared right into my eyes, again smugly. It was a look I was beginning not to like. "The question is, did Nathan forgive you?"

I collapsed back in my chair away from her probing look only to notice she wasn't the only one giving me one. Clay's eyes were locked on me, looking past Mike from the other end where the game of hostile takeovers was happening. "He doesn't know," I muttered, distracted.

There was a collective groan from either side of me. The sound was genuine, not faked or learned.

"Yep," I muttered silently, and then added my own groan. He didn't know, and there was a part of me, a large part of me, that wanted to keep that transgression quiet. The second one needed to be buried in a deep hole with a mountain of granite on top of it, but the constant gaze that was raping me from the other end of the deck told me there was always a threat it would rise from the grave.

"So do we need to give you the talk now that you are a grown woman, I mean," Apryl fake coughed, "witch?"

Feeling saved, I took the open door to change the subject. "Ah, no. Plus, I don't think you are equipped to do that." I had another witty comeback to add but paused to consider if it was safe to go there, and if it would bring me any safety. It was the only hope I had for my own sanity and future happiness. "Do we need to give you the talk? How are things with Clay?"

Her reply, the smack heard around the world, which she followed up quickly with an apology and rubbed where she hit me on the arm. It stung, but not too bad. I had no doubt it was good-natured. She laughed when she did it. The little tap didn't stop me from digging some more. This time, I lowered my voice and leaned over toward her.

"So, what is going on there?"

"Nothing," blurted the queen of denial. She couldn't blush, but she still squirmed. It was too automatic to not be authentic.

So far be it from me to be a smartass. "So, how is nothing going?"

That produced a little giggle from Apryl, and a surprised look from Jennifer, who pulled her seat closer for the detailed girl talk that would dominate much of the night. The giggle was my life preserver, my hope. If Clay and Apryl were clicking then he wouldn't keep pursuing me. The look he was still giving me gave me worry.

Apryl didn't spill too many details on what was happening with her and Clay. It was hard to tell if there was really anything more than just a budding interest, and one thought that occurred to me earlier in the night seemed to be a likely spark to the beginning of whatever it was, at least from Apryl's side, lack of choices. Jeremy and Apryl got along fine, but it's more brother and sister, and from the first night I met them I saw that little spark between Jeremy and Pam that appeared to go up in temperature at the Christmas Tree Decorating Party. From the looks of it, it would not be cooling off anytime soon. At some point most nights, they could be found canoodling together away from the rest of us. I had to wonder who would be the first to test the charms on our doors. Brad was a tree of another color, and we all knew that.

Laura and Mike were an obvious match. There was just a way about them that screamed old couple. There was a comfort in how they moved and existed together, and in some ways, recent events excluded. I felt Nathan and I were slipping into that.

That just left Clay as the only option for Apryl, if she felt the desire for someone else in her life. That was, unless she did what I did and cross the lines. My mind played around with the various combinations and the disasters that would result. There was Jack, and that was a no before it even started. It appeared no one, other than me, really took the time to get to know him. I remembered back to what he mentioned once about the distrust everyone had towards him because of what he could do. I could see that as a true barrier for him. The dog pack was a flat no. It just wouldn't work. Elsewhere in the world, vampires and werewolves were mortal enemies. A fact that is prominent in every movie I have ever seen or book I have read. After seeing how things were here, I had to ask and confirmed that fact with Rob and Jennifer separately. Both said it was true, but both also stated it would probably never be true for them, at least not with the ones here in the coven. Nurture over Nature it would seem.

As the night went on, and after watching Apryl and Clay share several close dances together, I found it easier to relax. The ascension was behind me, and that was a good thing. The vibration was still there, just below everything else I sensed. In my moments of absolute tranquility, where my thoughts no longer danced a wild gyrating jig—which wasn't often, I felt its purpose. The entire world buzzed, but not just in a buzz. The buzz had shape, texture, size, and magnitude. It radiated off, around, and through everything in the world. It was as if I could feel the fabric of the world itself. Each vibration was a wrinkle that traveled that fabric, and being telekinetic, I had to wonder. Could I yank on a thread of that fabric?

My mind was diving deeper into the meaning, and what I had to assume was a heightened level of awareness, when I felt the fabric of the world rustling. I didn't turn around from my place at the railing. This was my peaceful place. A place I had visited often to just stand with my thoughts and look out at the world. Tonight, I just want to look out without my thoughts.

"Larissa?" Clay asked very tentatively and sweetly. I turned to see him standing there alone, with the rest of the group on the other side of the deck, and Apryl hovering over the top of the Monopoly game that had all appearances of becoming very heated. More than a few hostile funds collections had occurred through the course of the game.

"Hey, Clay." I leaned back against the railing, full of dread

"I just wanted to say I was really sorry about earlier. I don't normally have a temper, but right now, it's..." he seemed to struggle for the word to say.

"Hard? Not feeling yourself?" I offered, hopefully giving him an out on many levels.

"In more ways than I can count. And it's not just about earlier with Nathan. It's also about last night. That was out of line, and I need to apologize," he said contritely.

"You don't need to." I caught myself slipping back into the role of counselor. With all that had happened. I couldn't do that for him, especially not now, though with things feeling like that might be righting, a little, I didn't want to just cut him off completely. One little piece of advice to send him on his way wouldn't hurt. "It's part of being a newborn. You can go from as cool as a clam to on fire in the blink of an eye. It will take time for that to level out, and for you to learn how to control it a bit. Just like we talked about last night. Don't expect too much from yourself now. Okay?"

"Yep." he leaned against the railing next to me and looked out at the same beauty I had been admiring. At least he did at first. Then I both felt and watched his head dip and his eyes closed. Mine followed. He wasn't leaving. "It's just so hard right now. You said it right last night. I am just the passenger, as all these things happen." His head shook from side to side.

"You will know when it is time to try and take the wheel. For now, just absorb and get used to how you feel. Then you will be able to figure out how to manage it." That was the same advice I had tumbled around in my own head before he walked up. I needed to feel the world, and what it was telling me now. What to do it with, if anything, would be a later step. He didn't show any signs of leaving, and I thought about walking away myself, I should have.

"Will I? How did you know?"

"Clay," I started, trying to think of the best way to let him down easily, which was not a skill I had. Blunt and forward, that was me. If I could soften it any at all, that would be an achievement for me. "Look, I know you have a lot going on, but," I paused to play the next sentence out in my head. It was about as soft as a sledgehammer, but it was the best I could do. "With everything that has gone on between us, I am not sure I am the best person to give you advice. Why not talk with Apryl, and Mrs. Bolden?"

He turned toward me, and his hand brushed my arm and my body melted, just that quick. My drug was back, and my body was fully accepting this hit, and already wanting another. The administering hand ran down my arm to my wrist, and wrapped its fingers around it, giving me a super charged dose. "Because it's you I need."

I needed to pull away from him, but wanting and needing are two different things, and with how I was feeling, want was winning. "I am not the best person to help you right now," I forced out past the pure ecstasy I felt.

"You seem to have everything right-as-rain, Miss Dubois." It was an odd phrase for someone that age, but that wasn't what caught me off guard. There was something about the voice. Something that resembled someone else, but it had to be my mind playing with me. Even odder, Clay shook his head, as if feeling some kind of discomfort.

"You okay?"

The look he returned was a leer at first, and then it became confusion, followed by another shake of the head. Both of his hands rushed up to his temples and rubbed them rather aggressively. I moved down the rail to give him space. Well, it was really to give me space. Something was bubbling through me, and I was concerned I might throw him over the railing.

"Larissa, I am sorry. I am not sure…" Clay started a rather pained sounding apology. I didn't wait for him to finish it, and walked away back toward the others, but he made a mistake that Nathan only had a few times. He reached and grabbed me by the hand, yanking me backward. "Wait!

I spun around to look him right in the eye as I yanked my hand from him. I wanted him to know he crossed the line, and it needed it to be loud and clear, but when I saw his sullen expression and felt the trembling in his hand. I couldn't. Not because I was thinking of him as a counselor at that moment. No, I was thinking of Clay as a person, and me as another person that could do something right now that would hurt him, and that wouldn't accomplish anything. "Don't leave." He reached for me again, this time not threatening, and the tremble in his voice matched the one I felt in his hand.

"You are the one person up here I feel a connection with. There is something special." The fingers of his hand slowly rubbed my hand, much the same way Nathan did, and that sensation was back, but it wasn't able to control me this time. Adrenaline and a good bit of my temper, had a blockade setup

"Clay, I have a boyfriend. You know that, and you have Apryl." I broke my focus on Clay just long enough to check to make sure there were no prying eyes looking in our direction. So far, they were still consumed with the game, and enjoying how much Mike sulked.

Clay did the same, but his gaze was only at Apryl, and the grip on my hand loosened. His head dipped and he let out a half-hearted, "Yea." I felt he was going to let go of my hand all together, but his fingers slid between mine, and I yanked my hand back before he tightened his grip.

"Clay, you need to stop."

"I know, but I can't help but wonder. I feel such a connection. Something I don't with anyone else. I can't shake the feeling there is a reason I was found and brought here, and that reason was you." I couldn't shake the longing of his voice, but I couldn't entertain the notion. That I was about to discount if there was a master plan for us all, just this interpretation of it.

"Clay," I started and then slowed myself down. I needed to be careful about how I responded. "You're very sweet, and I can understand what you are feeling. I am here to help you, but don't mistake any gratitude or sense of caring you are feeling at the moment because of that as anything more. Your emotions are firing faster than your mind can handle right now. Give yourself time and things will become clearer, plus I think you have a genuine connection with Apryl. I have seen it. Just give yourself some time."

His only reply was to stand there and fidget nervously. I was right, and he knew it. Every little emotion he felt was at the extreme end of the spectrum right now. I hoped this was him realizing it. Either way, I felt the best move was to remove myself from the equation for a bit and leave. Just before I descended the stairs, I looked back. Clay had walked back over to the group, and Apryl had climbed on top of him in a chair. I hoped anything he felt for her was real, and not just an emotion run-amok. I didn't want to see her hurt.

21

The next day was Monday. The start of a new week. New beginnings. That was a thought that consumed me on so many levels. I had put my latest blow-up with Nathan in perspective, not that I was going to tell him that, yet. He needed to learn, and I was going to let him dangle a little more just to make sure. Though he might believe he was already off the hook after he waited for me outside my ascension. Then there was that.

Overall, things just felt different, and it was way beyond the light vibration that was still there, and a surprise kidnapping told me that was not something that was particular to me. I hoped what had happened with Clay was behind me as well. Seeing him snuggled up with Apryl was a good sign for that, but I had decided to take a safety measure and enact a policy of avoidance for the time being.

Nathan and I were walking through the door of Mr. Markinson's class when Lisa grabbed me by the arm, yanking me back out through the door. "Relax Nathan, she is okay. This is girl stuff," she said as she rushed me the opposite way down the hall and into the library. Inside the door she pinned my shoulders against the wall, but not in a threatening way. This was a playful side I hadn't seen from her before.

"So, how do you feel?"

"Fine," I said.

"Come on. You don't feel different somehow?" She winked at me.

Mrs. Tenderschott's warning played in my head as I realized what she was asking, and that gave me an easy out that shouldn't create any problems. "We really aren't supposed to talk about this."

"No, we aren't supposed to talk about what we experienced with those that haven't. No one said anything about not talking about what we felt with those that have," she said, still smiling and losing a bit of the dark edge Lisa normally projected. She was right. "I have to know. Does everything feel different? Clearer?"

"Yep," I agreed, both to her point about no one saying we couldn't talk about what we felt after, and about how I felt. "Everything vibrates," I added, curious to see what her response was.

"Thank God," Lisa said, letting go of my shoulders. "So, I wasn't crazy. That insane vibrating kept me up the entire night until it all but went away in the morning. Lucky you, you didn't need sleep."

"It still got on my nerves though until I think I figured out what it was."

"The world around us?" Lisa asked.

When I nodded, her face exploded into the biggest smile I had seen. "Once you figured that out, did you feel a sense of clarity and responsibility that you hadn't before? That things you once worried about before were no longer as important."

"Exactly, but I couldn't put my finger on why."

"It's like someone flipped a light switch," remarked Lisa.

I couldn't have described it better myself. That was exactly what it was. Neither of us could explain to the other why, we just had to assume it was part of the ascension. Not for the obvious reason, either. We had both reached the same conclusion, and it was rather cliché. With great power comes great responsibility. Our ancestors wouldn't grant us one without the other.

When we returned to class, I took my seat next to Nathan and Lisa went to her normal seat at the table. Our newest student was sitting there in my old seat next to Apryl introducing himself. Seeing Clay there was a little surprising. We were only two days removed from his little incident, but I didn't notice anyone that appeared to be afraid of him, which should go a long way with calming any fears he had about how his first impression went. I myself would keep a watchful eye just in case I needed to intervene, while keeping my distance.

After class, Nathan and I were the last to leave. I tried to leave first, like we normally did. Our table was at the back. Nathan seemed to have other ideas and held me back by the arm and allowed everyone else to walk past us. His grip was a little firmer as Clay passed, something I chose to ignore. For now. He had released his hold when we reached the door.

"Larissa, got a second?" Jack asked, and I could hear Nathan sigh.

In the grand scheme of things, this was nothing to blow up about, but he needed to learn, so his little exhale earned him a stern look. His reply, "More girl stuff?"

"Yep." This time I grabbed Jack and led him down to the library, leaving Nathan behind us.

Inside, I didn't pin him to the wall like Lisa had me. Instead, I entered calmly and placed my books down on the closest table and turned and leaned back against it. I was hoping this wasn't the start of a long progression where each of the witches were going to grab me and pull me some place to talk. Lisa was different. She knew. The others are probably curious as hell since their turns are coming in the next few months, with Marcia being two years away. "What is it?"

"Are you okay?"

If I could have sighed, I would have. So, I faked it and then rolled my black eyes to add to the message of frustration. "Jack, I'm not sure if they have explained it to you or not, but I can't tell you about it. Mrs. Tenderschott was very clear about that."

Jack was already shaking his head in response. "Not that. I mean Jean St. Claire. Last night was not like any of the others."

"Other what?" I shot back.

"Visits."

"Jack, he didn't visit me last night." I was going to tell Jack I had only had one visit from Jean St. Claire since I put up the runes, and after that I reapplied them and there was nothing since, but he interrupted me.

"He had to have. Last night, or rather early this morning. I felt how upset you were, how painful it was. It was loud and clear, and just like the other times."

I stood there shaking my head no as Jack emphatically told me what he felt. "Why do you assume every major emotional outburst you feel has something to do with me? Do I seem that unstable? Wait, don't answer that." I might have slapped him if he had.

It was impossible, I explained. Jean never showed, and as far as I knew, he didn't even make an attempt. If he did, I didn't feel it, and definitely not as strong as Jack believed, but while I replayed the night in my head just to make sure I hadn't glossed over something in my ascension glow, there it was. Well, not exactly, but it could explain what Jack felt. It wasn't me, and it had nothing to do with Jean St. Claire, but there was someone in anguish, Clay. For a few moments, while we stood at the railing, he appeared really upset, and even made a harsh comment to me, which I walked away from. That could have pushed him further into that emotional hole he was feeling. "Are you feeling okay?" I humorously asked, though it appeared I was the only one who got the joke. "It wasn't me, and it wasn't Jean."

Jack jerked back before he asked me, "Come again?"

"It wasn't me, and it wasn't Jean. It was Clay. That's twice." I held up two fingers on my left hand while Jack completed his headshake. He still seemed to be in denial. I explained further, "Clay is really struggling. Inside, he has feelings and emotions that are pulling him apart. Primal urges that fight with whom he is. Depression over the loss of his life and what he is now, and hatred for all he has done. He seemed to be struggling last night and let a comment slip, and I walked away from him. You probably felt that. I can't even imagine how intense his emotions are at the moment."

Jack's eyes left me and searched around the room while his mind processed what I had just told him. There were no direct questions or attempts to deflect any of what I had said. Not that he could have. It was the only explanation, and the more I thought about it, it was technically my fault. I should have stayed there and tried to help him more. He touched a nerve, and I let my emotional instability control my next move. Maybe that ascension hadn't made me as enlightened as I had thought.

"Well maybe. This is the second time." he finally remarked, but he didn't sound completely convinced.

"It has to be." I left the table and walked to Jack, remembering some of the cues from class. I leaned forward and placed my hand on Jack's shoulder. There was no flinch. "Trust me. I haven't had any run-ins with Jean since I reapplied the runes. If I had, I would tell you."

Now he was looking into the dark orbs of my eyes, and his apprehension melted away. "Must have been it. I can't believe I have been wrong twice." There was a hint of his normal sarcastic tone. "It must have been intense."

"It was." I didn't dare go into what it was about, and stood there hoping to God Jack didn't take notice of how uncomfortable just thinking about it made me.

"It must have been. You are a nervous wreck." Jack relaxed back against the wall, and crossed his arms. "What happened, exactly?" The knowing look told me he knew the emotions involved and just needed me to fill in the details.

Jack stumbled to the closest chair after I told him what happened. "Nathan is going to kill him."

I couldn't disagree. He would if he ever found out. "Nathan is never going to know. Got it?"

"Yep," agreed Jack with a swallow. "I just have one question."

"What?"

"I make a little comment and get tossed in the pool. He did all that and you didn't do anything to him."

"What was that about?" Nathan asked when we emerged from the library. I didn't hesitate to tell him exactly what we talked about, well not everything. Nathan stopped where we were in the hallway and asked me again if Jean had come to visit me, but I assured him, just like I did for Jack, he hadn't. He would be the first to know if there were any visits. We were at the door of our next class when Nathan made a comment that really summed up how Clay probably felt better than I could have. "It must be hell to hate what you are."

That statement got me thinking a little. Did I hate what I was? It wasn't a question I could answer with an unequivocal yes or no; it wasn't that easy. Did I hate what happened? Absolutely. It robbed me of so much, in essence, my life. But, as much as it took from me, it gave me something in return. A life that I would have never had a chance to know. The opportunity to live an eternal life. My physical abilities. Not to mention the people who were part of my life. The Nortons, Mrs. Tenderschott, Mrs. Saxon, Jennifer and Kevin Bolden, my friends—which I really felt I could call them that now, Amy, and Nathan. I couldn't forget that. Who knows if I would have met anyone like him if this hadn't happened? But, I seriously doubted it. It was difficult to imagine ever feeling this way about anyone else. Halfway through Mrs. Saxon's class I realized that I had found a peace with what I was now, and the unity of the two worlds I was part of. That wasn't to say, I was happy being something most of the world considered a dark creature from hell itself, but I knew that wasn't me.

In Mrs. Saxon's spells class, there was a change of the seating arrangement that I wasn't prepared for, nor did I approve of. I had enjoyed having the back table all to myself to work on the spell or ability of the day, and lately being out of the eye shot of everyone was great. I didn't really want them seeing how easily I was doing everything while they struggled. Today was no different. I knew what we were going to cover. Mrs. Saxon told us on Friday and asked us to read up on it over the weekend, as this was a bit more than just hand magic, as Mr. Demius would call it. I flipped through it and found it was the closest trick in the book to the symbols and the other types of magic that I was told were not to be taught. I wasn't sure how Mrs. Saxon was going to pull this one off in class, though. We needed a target, living, and there was one un-negotiable rule in her class, we were not allowed to try anything on one another, and God knows Gwen has tried to bend the rule more than a few times. Freezing someone, really suspending time around them, was going to be hard to do without someone to suspend time around, unless this was a purely lecture based class, but that went against her other rule. All lessons were practical skills focused, meaning we were to learn by doing. My only question I had from the reading, who in the Harry-Potter-hell decided to name it subsisto, the Latin word for stop. Couldn't they be more original than that? I guess it could be worse, freezioso.

I hadn't tried it on my own over the weekend yet, for the same aforementioned reason that I wondered how we were going to do it in the class, but I had done it under the supervision of my mother almost a century ago. The target, Mr. McCoy, a fellow witch, who was more than happy to assist. The man was either an idiot or had a ton of confidence in me. I tended to lean toward idiot. He didn't bat an eye as he stood in the parlor while my mother gave me all the warnings about losing concentration while doing this. It had me weirded out so much I even told my mother I didn't want to and even started crying. She kept encouraging me, and he stood there ready. When I finally started the words, which this time she said were more than just for show, my voice cracked. "Time comes. Time goes."

She grabbed my hands and held one above the other. I allowed the sand she placed in my top hand to slip through my grip and fall to the bottom hand, and together we recited, "Like the sands of time, it continues to move." Then my top hand squeezed off the stream. The chipper, white-haired gentleman who stood in the center of the round rug in our parlor froze where he stood. His hand mid-retreat from a brush of his white bushy mustache.

When I loosened my grip and allowed the sand to trickle through again, his hand made it back to his side and he looked to my mother for confirmation that the spell had been successful. I remembered; this was my first what I would really call a witch's spell. It wasn't until later that my mother told me her most dire warning. While I could hold someone in that state for as long as I wanted just by holding the sand, and I could even hold them indefinitely by putting the sand down some place, I must never throw the sand away. That act, she said, would erase them.

That was a frightening statement for a ten-year-old to hear, and even more so to imagine what that actually meant. I became scared of the spell, only performing it under the supervision of my mother, and only once without her hands guiding my own. That was a little more unnerving than I could handle. I was afraid I would drop the sand. I still knew how to do it, and I had no doubts I could perform it on demand now. Now, I could even create the sand, thanks to a few symbols, but I couldn't let anyone else know that.

I had to wonder if it were the prospects of what Mrs. Saxon might let us try that was behind Gwen's new selection of seat, and that wide smile on her face as I took my normal seat, which was now right next to her. It was moments like this that made me question how far we had really buried the hatchet. We were friendly, and at times even more so, as she was curious and needed some help. Other than the one time where I attempted to help everyone with compulsion, her requests were normally done in private, and her new seat could be another attempt to obtain my help with something that she feared she would struggle with. My observation of Gwen was she was a really good witch and could do most everything, when she put the time in that is. Her problem was, frustration set in too quickly, causing her to become discouraged. Something I used to be able to relate to all too well.

"So, I have a question." Gwen asked before Mrs. Saxon started her class. The look on her face was the normal serious look she gave when she needed my help with something. This was playful, almost flirty. Then an oh-no-not-her-too thought flashed across my mind, and I wondered If I was going to spend the next few days fending off attempts to ask questions about the ascension. Gwen was next, so her curiosity made sense.

"Gwen, I can't talk about it." I looked at her knowingly. "You know that, right?"

"Oh, yeah," she responded, stunned. "I do, and it's not about that. It's about Clay."

What was it Jack said? Complicated? He wasn't kidding. "What about Clay?"

"What's he like?"

I had no clue why she batted her eyelashes at me. It was all I could do not to laugh, which wasn't my first impulse. That one involved emptying the contents of my stomach, if there were any.

I gave her the obvious answer. "He's a vampire. Remember? The Christmas party?" To help clarify for her blondeness whose vision was obviously impaired by the glaze that was across her eyes as she talked, I also reminded her of when I put him against the wall and Mr. Bolden led him away after trying to attack one of her, our, friends.

"I know that, but is he nice?"

That was something I was still on the fence with. He was nice, I guess, but I was starting to pick up on something *off* about him. At times he was nice. At times he was rather hostile, aggressive, and off, that was really the best word for it. What was worrying me more at the moment was, why she was asking. That goofy grin on her face, and those star-crossed eyes told me this was going to be more than just complicated. This was something that could lead to all-out war.

Apryl already had her sights, if not her hooks, set on Clay. That was her pair. Of course, Clay had a say in it too, and I hoped, prayed even, that what I saw when I left the deck last night was a sign that he had finally given up on what even he was pursuing with me and realized how Apryl felt about him. She had given him more than a few subtle hints. Most every moment she saw him walking around or sitting alone, she was quick to join his side.

If Gwen was going to do what I think she was, she wasn't just going to upset the apple cart. She was going to flip it over, chop it up, and set it on fire, and that wouldn't be good for anyone. I had to defuse this bomb before it went off, and at all costs, all while avoiding any appearance of favoritism. If Gwen knew I was trying to protect Apryl, that might be enough to pull the hatchet we buried right out of where ever proverbial hatchets are buried. There was a part of me that even sympathized with her. I got it. Her options were limited, too. If you looked at the vampires, things had evened up. Whether that was just a random happening, or part of some big master plan that we were all just actors in, I didn't know and I had enough on my plate to try to understand to even ask; there might be an answer out there for me if I did. There was only one male on the witch side and that was Jack, and I didn't see that happening. There was a hint of him and Marcia at Mrs. Saxon's Christmas tree decorating party, but that was all it was, a hint, just a spark. But who knew where that would lead? The remaining options almost made me laugh. The dog pack enjoyed poking fun at Gwen as much, if not more, as any of us did. Martin was the worst of all, but then I had to wonder. Does he protest too much?

"He's nice," I answered, leaving it simple, and enjoyed watching the queen deflate a bit as I didn't divulge more before Mrs. Saxon placed two bags of sand on our table and gave each of us a curious gaze. Now this was going to be complicated, I thought.

22

There was no breaking of the rules in Mrs. Saxon's spell class, but there was a slight bending of them. We weren't allowed to try our new trick on each other, and we absolutely weren't unsupervised. Just like how my mother taught me over a century ago, Mrs. Saxon kept a firm grip on each of our hands to make sure we controlled the sand properly, squeezing the stream off and then allowing it to restart a few seconds later. When it was my turn, I noticed the death grip she had on my hands until I witch-whispered to her, "I know." She loosened her grip but didn't remove her hands. Not that she didn't trust me, but more for the others.

Our target, a very reluctant Mr. Markinson, who gave me a few shots when it was my turn. Each barb he threw my way about taking it easy on him and another humorous apology about whacking me around that night outside was met with an evil smile meant to make him feel uneasy. It seemed to work. He twitched slightly when I squeezed off the sand. With each of the others, Mrs. Saxon told them when to loosen their hand, which was probably when she relaxed hers enough to allow the sand to slowly flow again. With me, there were no verbal cues. I let it go when I was ready. When Mr. Markinson was back in the world of the moving, he gave me a quick point and a smile. I curtsied.

That afternoon, Mr. Demius asked me how the others did with Mrs. Saxon's lesson, and I gave him an accurate report. Most were able to handle it, except for Tera, who needed a second go. She was the first to go, and I felt she was probably nervous. It was a good thing Mrs. Saxon, like my mother, waited until afterwards to give us the big warning about dropping the sand. If she had told everyone that first, the pucker factor would have gone up significantly for everyone, including Mr. Markinson. Well, maybe not everyone.

That, as with anything else, had other uses, Mr. Demius explained, or tried to. What he said seemed so fantastical that even I had a tough time believing it. It was really out there, and disbelief must have been written all over my face. He grabbed me by the arm and led me to a spot on the floor and turned me toward a natural spring waterfall that ran down the wall in the corner. It wasn't there a few moments ago, but it was now. Then he proceeded to the other side of the room, where he wrote several runes in a circle. Celtic crosses dominated the rune, and I knew he was setting up a ring of protection. They were similar to the ones I used on the door frame in my room. He stood inside of it and told me to do exactly as he had described, and I did.

I positioned my hands just as I would have if I had had sand. Instead, I produced a little stream of wind that blew from one empty hand to the other. "Time comes. Time goes. Like the sands of time, it continues to move." I squeezed off the breeze, and then everything around me stopped. Even the vibration that had been with me since last night. It was all gone. I looked around and noticed the water falling in the waterfall was frozen mid-stream. Behind me, illuminated by light coming in through the skylight overhead, dust particles hung in the air. Just beyond the particles was a smiling Mr. Demius. Slowly, I let the wind return and the sound of running water again filled the room, just over the vibration of the world.

I finally looked up at the clock, not aware that I had just spent four hours in what I was calling my class of self-awareness, which was what it really had become. A safe place for me to experiment and experience all I was, all I could be, and all I should be. It was time for my favorite part of the day, and I rushed out to the pool area. Right past the gingerbread house, which brought a smile to my face when I spied it out of the corner of my eye, and the tree. The snowstorm inside had picked up, but it was no match for what was going on outside. Mother nature had thrown her own entry into the competition. The white majesty that covered the world for as far as you could see won out easily. Down the cleared path and under a snow dusted umbrella sat Nathan and Amy. Both bundled up for what was the coldest night so far. We probably needed to move our nightly ritual to the library until spring came, but not until tomorrow. Tonight, I had a different idea.

Without walking off the path, I lifted two loosely packed balls of snow and sent them slowly flying in their location. From where I stood, I had the perfect view. Nathan was the first to be hit, right in the back. Amy was laughing until her eyes exploded wide open when she saw the one I had intended for her, but I had another surprise in store for her. The snowball stopped just in front of her and turned and went back to whack Nathan right in his beautiful face. It wasn't a hard hit. I didn't want to damage his gorgeous features.

Amy's laughter echoed against the outside of the coven, and I watched as Nathan stood up looking around for his attacker, but I was gone long before he turned in my direction. When he finally saw me, I had Amy in my arms, as almost a human shield, and I was helping her create her own to toss at Nathan. Her arm didn't have the strength to get it that far, but I gave it a little extra help in that regard to make sure it found its target. To be a good sport, I didn't interfere with any of his throws our way, and I didn't rush Amy away. If it was going to hit us, it hit us. Surprisingly, Amy laughed even harder when we were hit than when ours hit Nathan.

Above us, a host of witches, vampires, shapeshifters, and werewolves were leaning over the railings on their outside balconies. I motioned for them to come on down, too. In mere seconds, the railings were empty, and our assault on Nathan had ended with a new unspoken alliance formed. In the time it took the others to make it outside, we had amassed a rather large pile of snowballs and were sitting at the ready for the first person to poke their head out. Poor Martin, he never saw the volley coming, but he took it in good nature, dropping to the ground and rolling around in the snow until he came up firing himself. Then it was on. All-out war, no teams, no alliances, no cliques. We were just teens being teens, and it felt good, even for this old broad.

Everyone attacked everyone, and it was all in good fun. Even Clay seemed to have a good time. He was smiling, something he didn't do often, but something he should. It was nice looking. Not that I would ever admit that in front of Apryl, but I could see why the others, including Gwen, would be smitten by him. Remembering the recent conversation between myself and the queen of pink, which she was covered in from head to toe, I made a cautionary check, Apryl wasn't far from Clay's side, just a few feet from me, and Gwen was on the other side of the pool being pummeled by snow from all directions. Payback is a bitch, and it looked like she had it coming for years.

Most of my and Amy's attacks were at Nathan and the other vampires. Though she nailed Jack on the back once in what appeared to be an accident when she was aiming at Mike. To spread the wealth, I grabbed Amy and headed around the pool behind Steve and Stan, the two brothers, and let them have it. Both brushed off the sneak attack and then gave chase to Amy. Even the ever-quiet Cynthia joined in on the chase. I had always hoped she would be something of a sister to Amy, being that they were close to the same age and the only girls in the shapeshifter floor. It was nice seeing them playing together.

Who was not nice to see playing together was Clay and Nathan. Somehow, in the couple of minutes I had slipped away, Clay had moved closer to Nathan. To everyone else, it looked harmless. Two teenage boys lofting snowballs as far and as fast as they could. To me, this looked like trouble. The smiles each had when I last saw them were gone, and the looks that replaced them were not shared. Clay had a devious stare, focused on his target and never looking at Nathan while he spoke to him almost out of the side of his mouth. Nathan's grimace was more irritated, and his eyes cut back and forth between his targets and Clay.

I moved to insert myself back into the equation but did so with a snowball to make it less obvious what I was doing. It landed between them, producing two startled reactions, and drawing a snowball in response from only one of them. The other, Clay, rejoined his pair several feet away, but his gaze, make that his leer, never left me.

Nathan lobbed another at me before I joined his side and helped send a few Gwen's way and then took aim at Martin, Robert, and Steve, who were sending them over in rapid fire. There was no way to avoid or dodge them. We just had to brace for impact and then return fire once the cloud of snow fell as it broke apart when it hit us.

"Interesting guy there," Nathan remarked with all the sarcasm in the world. Then he sharpened that sarcasm and threw a real dart in my direction. "Then you should know that. Sounds like you and he have quite the conversations at night." His tone both stung and pierced me right before he walked away.

"Don't start!" I followed right behind him around the pool. Balls of white, fluffy snow zinged past us. He only paused long enough to return fire when one hit him. "It isn't whatever your mind is constructing." It was probably worse, but I wasn't going there. "Jennifer has me helping him just like her and Kevin had helped every other vampire that has come through this place for the last several years. Think of it as training so I can help out." I explained as we walked past Laura and Pam, prompting two curious glances. It was almost like they had never seen two people fight before, and with the way Nathan was stomping across the snow-covered deck, it was clear that is what this was. "Nathan, stop," I requested, not liking how whiny my voice sounded.

He stopped. Now what? I didn't have a bloody clue. The convenience of what I had just relearned crossed my mind. I sure could use the extra time.

"So, you are supposed to stay within your own kind?" He asked and turned around to face me. Nathan's quiet confidence was just a lost memory. The person before me was sullen. His eyes were wide with oceans of white almost swallowing his blue irises I so enjoyed getting lost in; now their appearance broke me. "Vampires should be with vampires. Isn't that right? It is better that way, right?"

"No!" I responded, and tried to think of something else to say, but my mind was making another leap. Nothing else was needed to deny that. It wasn't my belief and was so absurd it didn't need anything further. That would just let the idea live longer, and it needed to die. The thought that something else needed to die boiled deep inside me, and it was bubbling up to the top quickly. "Who said that?" I demanded rhetorically as I turned my head toward Clay.

Clay never saw me coming. Neither did Gwen, who was standing next to him doing the best she could to get his attention. I stepped right between them interrupting her mid-sentence. I felt her reach for me. I wasn't sure if she was just going to give me a polite tap on the shoulder or grab me to be more forceful with her protest over my interruption, but I didn't care. I put my hand behind me where she could clearly see it and the glowing ball in my palm. If she wanted some, I would give it, but I hoped she would step back. My problem wasn't with her now. It was with Clay. "What the hell, man? What did you just tell my boyfriend?" There was a stunned silence, then the sounds of several people scampering in the snow. They were moving away. "You heard me. So, tell me, what did you tell my boyfriend?"

Clay didn't answer and stared back at me blankly.

"You heard me. I know you did." I was now just inches from his face, and his silence was turning up the burner on that boiling inside. "Hey Gwen," I called back without moving an inch to face her blondeness in her pink snow suit. "Did you know this guy thinks everyone should stay with their own kind? Vampires with vampires. Witches with witches. I guess werewolves with werewolves and shapeshifters with shapeshifters. Do I have that right, Clay?" His name was elongated leaving my tongue, as was the silence that stood between us until I saw a devious smile creep across his face. I am not one to be weirded out by a moment, not with all I had seen, but even I had to back up when he nodded. "You can have any opinion you want, but keep it to yourself..."

Apryl stepped in between us and interrupted my speech. There was a quick glare over my shoulder at Gwen, and I sensed something. Was it possible I was developing Jack's talent? Stepping back, I reached back and grabbed Gwen's hand. She didn't resist, which told me she sensed it, too.

"Back off Larissa. Clay just made a mistake," pleaded Apryl, as she turned to wrap her arms around him. I knew that she was trying to defuse the situation before detonation. She was looking at me as her friend and doing to Clay what Nathan did to me from time to time. His embrace was a magical one to calm me down in an instant, but there was something wrong. Her embrace didn't seem to have the same effect, and Clay's nostrils flared, even though he doesn't breathe.

"Larissa," croaked Gwen from behind, and I released her hand that I was squeezing a little too tightly, but I didn't let it go completely, and led her away.

"It is true, you know." The voice that said it had lost its smooth southern edge. It was a grater, and I was the cheese, and it shredded every sense of control I had.

Now it was Gwen's turn to strengthen her grip on my hand. She knew what was about to happen and used everything she had to hold me back. I tried to yank away as I stepped toward Clay, but God love her, at that moment, Gwen didn't let go.

"It absolutely is not." I was seething, much like he was the first night I met him. If I had been a cartoon, steam would be blowing out of my ears. Instead, I stood there, leaning as far as I could toward him, with Gwen pulling me the other way. My free hand balled up in a fist with every thought of what I could do with that one hand going through my head trying to decide which would do the most damage, but nothing matched what I wanted, and I gave up and walked away.

"You felt it when we kissed. You know you did. It's how it is supposed to – "

I heard the tree Clay landed against out in the forest crack and fall to the ground. That was the only sound, other than a silent "yes" from Jack.

23

"I didn't kiss him!" I exclaimed for probably the twentieth time since Nathan and I came inside to the privacy of his own room. Something his mother didn't object to when we stormed in and through her apartment on the way toward it. This was not a conversation I wanted to have with an audience. Having it was bad enough as it was.

"So, you just landed on his face," Nathan yelled back, almost laughing. "I guess that happens all the time." He got up off his bed and began marching around the room. "That is it. It makes perfect sense. The earth shifted, and he landed on your face. That is how it always happens, doesn't it? Every time someone is caught kissing someone they shouldn't." He left the room and walked back out into the marble palace.

"He kissed me." I yelled through the door. I knew how stupid that sounded as soon as I said it. I had to wonder if that technicality ever worked in these cases.

I had already made every argument I could think of, including the truth, which all of them were. At least Nathan hadn't asked me yet why I didn't tell him when it happened. The answer to that was rather obvious. There was nothing else to say, nothing else to do, except to just sit here and wonder if this had ruined us. I sure hoped it hadn't. It couldn't. Nothing Clay said was true. We weren't better if we stayed with our own. Maybe it was my greater level of self-awareness I now felt, but that was wrong for so many reasons. The biggest one, we can't let what we are to define who we are. Who I was, was a better person with Nathan Saxon in my life. No matter what ever that was I felt every time Clay touched me.

That thought drove me to get up off his bed and walk out to where he stood in front of the large bank of windows. Nathan looked magical standing there, glowing in the moonlight. I had no words to speak. There were none left to say. So, I didn't. I just walked up behind him and wrapped my arms around his waist and buried my forehead in his back. There was no I'm sorry. I had said that already more times than I could count, and I wasn't sure about Nathan, but I knew I had tired of its sound. To be truthful, I had nothing to be sorry for besides where we were now.

Feeling his body relax into me, and his hands grab my arms and pull them tighter, was the first good sign over the last twenty minutes. It didn't announce my forgiveness, and I wasn't about to break the silence and ask. I would take what he gave. That was how we stood and watched the dog pack return from their sweep of the woods. We watched the snow gather on the sill of the window, a thin layer of ice crept across the glass, distorting the moonlight like a stained-glass window. We didn't feel the cold of winter's majesty. I didn't even feel the cold of my own presence. I just felt us, and he did too. We were in sync with the vibration of the universe.

"Do you have feelings for him?"

"No. Absolutely not."

"Larissa, the truth, please," Nathan begged. I felt his body tense up again, bracing himself for my answer. "He said you did." Hearing his voice trail off like it did drained me.

"No," I said. "And that is the truth." I should have left it with that, but Nathan asked for the truth, and at this point, every secret was another cut into our relationship, which seemed like it was bleeding out as it was. "What he was talking about is a physical feeling."

I had barely started when Nathan pulled away and spun around.

"Wait! Just listen! Please!" Now it was my time to beg. I put both hands on Nathan's firm chest to keep him from storming away. He looked all around the room, at every place, except me. "I can't explain it, but I think it is a vampire thing." Nathan pushed against me, but I held firm. "Wait! Something about each touch was intense. It's hard to explain, but that doesn't matter to me. It meant nothing to me." I took my hands off his chest and threw myself at him, wrapping both arms around him, and waited for his arms to give me that restoring embrace.

"Becky!" Jennifer yelled as she came in through the door. Her voice shattered what was turning into an image of perfect. "Larissa! Nathan!" Our presence at the window surprised her.

"What's wrong?" I let go of my death grip on Nathan and rushed over to Jennifer to inspect the scratches on her face.

"It's Clay. Something is wrong with him. He isn't himself."

I didn't wait for any further explanation before I took off and was out on the empty patio in a flash. Up above me on the deck, I heard loud voices, and rushed back inside and ran into Nathan standing at the bottom of the stairs staring up at the source of the sound.

"You stay down here." He didn't argue, but his mother and Jennifer beat me to the stairs and blocked my way up. My head screamed move, all the way up. Once they were on our landing, I rushed through the door and down the hallway ahead of them. On the roof, I found Mike and Jeremy wrestling with Clay on the ground. Mr. Bolden was kneeling off to the side. The fast-fading bruises on his face told of his part of the struggle.

Jack grabbed me before I took two steps. How he got up here would be a topic for another time. Why he was up here in the danger zone was my more immediate concern. He was concerned with neither, as he pushed me to the other end of the deck, "Larissa, you were right. It was Clay all along, but there is something else there."

"What?"

"I don't know."

I pushed Jack aside and walked over to the mass of humanity that now included Brad. Mrs. Saxon had sent Jennifer back down to get Rob to help, but a growling and biting dog would only escalate things more than they already were. That wouldn't solve anything.

"Get off of him!" I yelled. Laura and Apryl scattered. Pam moved even further back. The boys hadn't heard me, and I didn't care, or wait. With an extended hand, I pulled Clay out of the mass and floated him up in the air where I held him, spread eagled, over the edge of the deck.

"Well Larissa, I do declare." The voice I heard wasn't Clay's. That was clear, and now I knew what Jack meant and why he had been so confused.

"Shut it," I shot back. "Give me one reason I shouldn't end this right now."

"Because you couldn't kill an innocent person, now could you?" Right then Clay's head jerked down and he, his voice, cried, "Help! Get me down! Don't drop me!"

I looked at Mr. Bolden and asked. "Where did you find him?"

"Gulfport," he groaned.

"Clay, just relax. I am not going to hurt you." Then Clay changed again. The expression on his face stretched into a familiar, evil smile. Then it clicked. I knew exactly why Jack felt what he did, and he wasn't wrong. He was actually right. I also knew how to deal with this, but I also knew if I did it in front of Mrs. Saxon, there may be hell to pay, but what other choice did I have? I tossed Clay across the deck into a row of cushioned chairs and leapt on top of him before he had a chance. Then, in instinct, or what Mr. Demius might call mastery, I created a burning Solar Cross and Besom in the air in front of me and then forced them into Clay's chest.

He screamed as the symbols burnt into his cold flesh, but Mrs. Saxon screamed louder when she saw the symbols herself. I held a finger back to her and knew I would have to explain it later.

"Clay, I am sorry that hurt, but it will protect you."

He was still writhing in pain on the ground when I looked back at Jack who nodded. With my guard let down, I reached down and cradled Clay's head and rubbed the mass of hair out of his face. The electrifying effect of contact with Clay was gone, and the question of why ran free in my head.

"I am so sorry."

His hands reached and rubbed his chest where the symbols were still smoldering. "The voice is gone. How did you do that?"

"Old family secret." I glanced at Mrs. Saxon, who still didn't appear all too pleased. Thank God there was only one other witch up here to witness me using forbidden magic, and I knew Jack could keep his mouth shut. Clay struggled up to his feet but wobbled. Apryl helped him to the closest seat where she took up the job of providing care. The burn wounds on his chest were already healing. Behind us, the boys were laid out all over the deck, recovering from the struggle. Later, I would tell them never to send a boy to do a witch's work.

"Clay, I need to ask you something and I need you to be as detailed as you can. Did you see who turned you?"

He nodded.

"What did he look like?" I knelt in front of him.

"Dark hair. Pale skin. Kind of a pointy nose."

That description didn't help. It matched everyone on the deck, minus Mrs. Saxon and Jack. I had a hunch and needed to know if I, and Jack, were right.

"Jennifer, how did you find out about Clay?"

She didn't answer, and instead, looked at her husband to answer. He was still on the ground but had gathered himself enough to make it to his knees. "An old friend reached out and told us about a rumor they heard about a young vampire who was turned and left alone."

While he explained it, a book appeared in front of me. This was the second time it appeared in front of me since I had arrived here at the coven.

"Would this old friend have any connections to the New Orleans area?"

At first Mr. Bolden said, "No," but then there was a hesitant, "Yes, maybe. He is from that area."

I opened the book to a familiar page and held it up in front of Clay. He about jumped out of his skin, sending the chair he sat in skidding back several feet. That confirmed what I already knew. I didn't even need to ask who on the page he recognized. It didn't matter, but I knew who the voice was in his head. That forced what I thought was his new urges grabbing the wheel from him from time to time. It wasn't that at all. Someone truly was yanking the wheel from Clay, and I now knew who it was, and Jack did too.

"He is the door," I said, looking back at Mrs. Saxon. Jean St. Claire either turned Clay himself, or had someone turn him, and then used him as the doorway to get to me. Why? I didn't completely understand.

Now there were a few others that understood what I did, while the rest were still confused. Clay was the most confused of all. Only the long version of the story would help, so I started.

24

"I don't know about this," protested Clay. Why shouldn't he protest? We were sitting in Mrs. Tenderschott's classroom, he in the same chair I sat in many times, while she prepared a potion he was going to be asked to drink.

"I know the feeling," I whispered as Mrs. Tenderschott walked by to retrieve another ingredient. Clay heard me and shot a look in my direction. I forgot who and what he was for a moment. "Relax. I have been right where you are a lot. Mrs. Tenderschott won't let anything happen to you. I... I mean we, need answers."

She giggled as she pulled down the jar of brown coffee grounds. This wasn't going to taste good. That was why she used the coffee. I felt a little bad for Clay, that was, until the appearance of a second cup on the table gave me a sinking feeling. Mrs. Tenderschott pointed at it and then pointed at me.

"Um, why?" I protested.

"You wanted to go along for the ride. To see what he saw. So, you either need to perform it or drink it." She stepped back from the table and motioned for me to take her place, and that sinking feeling hit a new depth. Spells and hand magic I had no problems with. Even my forbidden symbols were becoming second nature, or dare I say mastered. Potions were something I hadn't even tried outside of class, and I do mean never. My mother never covered them with me, and I hadn't reached that class yet in the Orleans' Coven. So, this would be a first.

"I'm not sure," I said and stepped back and readied myself to take my spot at the table next to Clay.

"You can do this," Mrs. Tenderschott reassured me.

"Larissa, I trust you," voted Clay, though I wasn't sure how informed that vote was.

"Well, what's the worst that can happen?" Mrs. Tenderschott and I exchanged an uncomfortable look at that remark. I already knew what could happen, but I didn't need those thoughts distracting me, or it would. I took her place, and finished mixing the potion, which at this point really consisted of adding in the coffee, boiling it, and then straining it to remove any of the larger particles of the copper, cloves, sage grass, and ground up root. I pushed the cup toward Clay. "Drink it all. Once you begin to feel odd, just go with it. I will be right there with you. Oh, and ignore any of the large parts of the rats' tails."

He stopped with the cup halfway up to this mouth, "Rat tails?"

"Sorry, bad joke. There is nothing like that in it. Go ahead and drink it." I watched as he did and then saw his body sway back and forth in his chair. Jennifer and Mrs. Saxon grabbed him and helped his head down to the table. I wondered if I had looked like that each of those times I had downed something she mixed up.

"Now, this is the part you never saw." Mrs. Tenderschott grabbed my hand and placed it on Clay's head. "It is very important that you control your emotions while you're in there. Remember Reginald? It's a two-way door. If you keep your emotions in check, they may not even know you are there."

"Got it."

"Now repeat after me. Memories are the paths of our lives. There is only one stop and one end, but we can return to a place at any time."

I said those words, and with none of the wooziness I felt when I was the subject of the potion, I was there in the black void, with Clay. "All right Clay, I am here with you. Can you hear and see me?"

"Yes," he said, his hands reached out to explore the nothingness around me.

"Now think back to that day. Right when they grabbed you." It didn't take long until a dark road with closed stores and shops in either side replaced the nothingness. Two creatures stalked Clay from the darkness created by the shadows of the buildings. There were no working streetlights and no traffic on the road. Clay was aware they were there, and was walking fast while looking back over his shoulder every few steps. I was standing in front of him and was almost trampled when he took off running. He was fast, and it surprised me he made it as far as he did before they caught him and yanked him into the closest alley. His body crashed into a dumpster and then crumbled to the ground. Two more figures joined us. One male and one female. The female wasn't a vampire, she was a witch and not a one of us wanting to blend in with society witch. White dreads hung down to her waist, hiding most of her face. Black figures were tattooed on her dark arms all the way up to her tattered clothes. The energy and vibrations around her felt dark and heavy. This was black magic, voodoo. I had a feeling I would find that along this path. Mrs. Tenderschott believed that was how Jean St. Claire was opening the door to come visit me. Clay was just a different door. It made sense he would use a similar key.

"Stop right there Clay!" I had become so distracted with her appearance I had lost track of what I was here to do, and the vampire was about to sink his teeth in to Clay. It wasn't Jean, but that was okay. I didn't necessarily need it to be Jean. I could use a variation of what we were doing to do some poking around. I just needed Clay's memory to do it. If I had allowed them to bite him, he would have lost consciousness, and the memory.

I bent down next to him as he leaned over Clay, his menacing fangs just inches from their target. I placed both hands on the sides of his head. There was no resistance, no reaction. Just a bunch of hope that this would work. "Eyes are the portal to my world."

Bingo.

I was there in his head, rolling through his memories, like Miss Sarah Roberts had done to me weeks before. It was easier than I thought to control the flow of his memories. From the looks of it, Raul Snyder was part of Jean St. Claire's inner circle. Which also explained why his picture was on the page with Jean St. Claire in the book. Using this moment as a reference, I moved back and forth, visiting the grand house with the large ballroom and the dark, dank, stone lined room that Jean had taken me to during each of his visits. It wasn't until the day before Clay was turned that I found something that interested me. Raul standing there with miss white-dreads, and Jean St. Claire, meeting under the cover of darkness in the mildew covered stone room. They were talking, mostly out of ear shot, but I could make out a few words, including my name, or make that my last name, which Jean said with a hiss. He wanted to break me, destroy me, and make me leave the coven. That was clear from what he said. The passion in which he gave both demands was crystal clear. Each screamed, with his voice echoing off the walls.

Too bad they don't know how bad they failed at that.

"Drive her out into the open, then she will be ours," he said with an evil smile.

He turned to miss white-dreads and asked, "You can do this right? You can make her fall in love with him?"

She objected to his question and walked away. Jean laughed. I followed her as far as Raul's eyes did, while Jean ordered, "You need to plant information so that sad sap of a coven finds him."

"Already covered," agreed Raul, as he followed the strange woman. Then, right there in the extreme corner of his right eye, was a sight that sent a shriek through my head that echoed in this nothingness. Everyone turned to look in Raul's direction. That is everyone except the woman I saw chained to the wall, Mrs. Norton. She was thin and gaunt. It looked like she hadn't fed in weeks, but that wasn't the worst of it. A single beam of sunlight shined through a hole in the ceiling above, searing the flesh of her arm, the same spot, every day.

If I could have, I would have had Raul rush over and let her out, but it didn't work that way. I let Raul go, and even though I knew it didn't work that way, I still reached down and ripped his head off just for the hell of it while I screamed.

Clay was lying on the ground below him, screaming. I moved on to the witch and repeated the feat, disappointed that no great pleasure came from it, since neither would really be hurt. When the second head hit the floor, I stopped screaming, and I finally heard what Clay was saying. "They are coming. They are coming." Right then, I was forced out, and not on my own accord, either.

I stumbled around the table and toward the door. Mrs. Tenderschott was calling my name, but I ignored her and continued. Clay attempted to call out to me too, but he was too groggy from the trip, something I remembered well. Neither of them would be able to say anything to help me straighten things out in my head. Only I could, I hoped. Then another voice called out before I reached the door. It wasn't anyone that was physically in the room, but I knew whose mouth it came out of without even turning around.

How he was getting through the protection I had seared into Clay earlier I wasn't sure, but it appeared to be extremely painful to Clay. His body shook and writhed out of Jennifer and Mrs. Saxon's grip. He attempted to walk but couldn't and just flopped to the floor. But his eyes, those eyes, never left my face during the fall and the impact on the tile floor. They were no longer Clay's. Both were lifeless, but Jean's were colder, and had an evil slant.

I marched forward, wanting to kick them so hard to straighten out that slant, and I believed Jennifer knew what my intention was too. She stepped in the way and reminded me, "It's Clay! Larissa, it's Clay!"

"Did it upset you to see her hanging there?" he roared.

I clamped my mouth shut and stared straight into Jennifer's eyes. Her hands urged me to calm down, but there was only one way to release a spring under tension, and it wasn't slow or calm.

"So much pain. So much suffering. All on account of you, Larissa. Who else needs to suffer? Clay? Your witch friends?," his eyes shot over to Mrs. Saxon. "Or how about your human boyfriend? What a waste. Or that wonderfully precious little girl. What is her name? Oh yes, Amy."

Now Jennifer's hands were on me, holding me back. She was strong, though if I really pushed things, I could have tossed her aside like a rag doll. "No," she mouthed and shook her head. I relaxed and took a step back. She was right. Kicking the slant out of those eyes wouldn't fix anything. I sent another burning Solar Cross through Jennifer and into Clay's back. After the first one burnt in, there was a second, and a third, and a fourth. I only stopped when Mrs. Saxon grabbed my wrist to keep me from forming it.

I turned and walked out. Clay screaming in pain behind me. At least I knew it was Clay that was screaming. What I had done, I hoped, slammed the door shut on Jean St. Claire. Mrs. Saxon asked me to wait, but I didn't. This didn't involve her.

"He used a love spell to try to make me fall in love with Clay," I announced for all to hear as I hit the door.

25

To say I had made my mind up before I left the room would be like, well, a whole host of cliches. Reading the last page of a book first. The horse has left the barn. The race was over before it started. The end was a foregone conclusion. In my mind it was an open and shut case. There was no reason for a long drawn out debate, and as much as I hated to admit it, he was right. I had brought a lot of pain and suffering to those around me. I probably would continue to do so if I didn't change the course the world was heading, and I was the only one that could do anything about it.

Before I did it, I needed something. Something that might help me with this, so I ran upstairs to my room. I didn't give anything a second look. No long goodbyes, as I walked out the door with Mrs. Norton's note in my back pocket. This wasn't a goodbye. I was coming back if I survived.

I started down the stairs, where Mrs. Saxon stood waiting. She wasn't there to give me a sendoff. She had already started her argument about the dozens of reasons I couldn't take off, again. I didn't hear them. I didn't want to. Not a one of them mattered. This was something she couldn't understand. I mean, come on; she was just a witch, and this was so much more. This was also something very personal.

Jennifer joined her by the time I was at the second landing, and together they sounded like a chorus, singing the greatest hits of all the reasons I needed to calm down and think. Maybe I did, but unfortunately, neither of those tunes were on the playlist that was turned up to thirteen in my head.

I didn't feel any regret or worry as I moved both of them out of the way with a single flick of my wrist. That didn't stop the lecture, though. Some of the words were starting to get through, and they were getting personal now. The names of Nathan and Amy were the common starts of every phrase, and I would be lying if there wasn't a tug each time I heard them. What neither of those had realized, or if they had they were ignoring it—which I hoped to be the case because only an idiot wouldn't see it—if I didn't take care of this, there couldn't be a future with either of them in my life. That was a danger I wasn't willing to put either of them in, no matter how much it hurt.

The one phrase that stopped me dead in my tracks was a surprising one. Not that she said it, but that I reacted to it. "Larissa, you aren't ready yet. There is so much I still need to teach you."

That stopped me dead in my tracks, just a few feet short of the door out of the coven. When I spun around, I must have been growling or showing my fangs or something. Both women, who I had come to think of as my closest friends, were struck with fear. If my look wasn't bad enough, my words were the icing on the cake. "You have a lot to teach me? That's a laugh." I took another step toward the door.

"Larissa," Mrs. Saxon started. I recognized that tone. It wasn't the friend-tone. This was the stern teacher and headmistress tone. A lecture was blowing in. Unfortunately, she was about to run into a stronger front.

"What?" I didn't even turn around.

"He will kill you," she started. I wanted to fire back at her, but I didn't and placed my hand on the large brass door handle. "I don't doubt that at some time in the future you will have to face him, but not yet. There is so much..."

I spun and cut her off right there with a tone sharp enough to perform surgery. "Don't. Just don't say there is more I need to learn, or there is more you need to teach me. What? Do I need to learn a new way to light a candle? Maybe I can learn to make it rain and drown him? That is what we are covering in the next class, right? Controlling nature?" My hand slapped the center of my forehead, hard enough to be heard. "Oh, that's right. I forgot. He doesn't breathe. Maybe I can strike him with a lightning bolt. Wait, that won't work either. One hit me during the ascension and all I got was a little vibration. Whoa, scary stuff there. I am sure the three-hundred-year-old vampire from hell will just roll over and die at that." I made eye contact with both Jennifer and Mrs. Saxon before I continued my speech, which now had a wider audience. Mrs. Tenderschott had joined them, and Tera and Jack were out on their landings, taking it all in. Part of me was glad to see that. They needed to hear what I was about to say. After all, it was my responsibility to help restore witches to what they used to be. Isn't that what they asked me to do? "My mother taught me true magic, the old magic. The stuff the council doesn't want anyone other than them to know. The stuff that I doubt even you fully understand."

Mrs. Saxon surprised me at how quickly she whipped two flaming symbols in front of her and sent them to the door where the continuous lines of the infinity wrapped around both door handles and then locked together with a solar cross. Impressive. She knew a little more than I knew, and I regarded her with an appreciative, but mocking look. Her choice had an error though. The infinity didn't apply to the physical world, it applied to the soul. She should have used the sun, a circle with a dot in the center. The door wasn't any more secure than if she had tied it with tissue paper, but to be a good sport about it, I added to the show and waved my hands in the shape of an upside-down triangle while thinking of the symbol. A river of water fell from above the door and washed her ill-made lock away, cleansing and removing that negative impurity from my world.

I turned and curtsied, not expecting to be allowed to walk out the door without another attempt to stop me, and Mrs. Saxon didn't disappoint. This time, I never saw the symbol, if she had used one, but I heard the crashing of the rocks behind me forming a wall to block the door. "Larissa, wait. Let's talk this out." She almost broke me then.

It wasn't just a wall of rock, which I could have removed in any of more than two dozen ways. It was what was on them. Each rock had a rune written on it. A charm, to lock it in place, and she wrote it for this purpose. There was the normal solar cross that is used for protection or locking something in or out, that was expected. Even seeing what looked like a loaf of bread wasn't out of place as it represented the protection and continuous life. She trying to keep me from doing something that would endanger my life. What I didn't expect was the half circles of the sunrise and sunset. One faced up and the other faced down. They had opposing meanings, but I knew what they meant when they were used together. I needed to release the guilt and pain I felt. Only when I had done that would the rocks disappear. She knew me well enough to know those emotions were what was driving me now.

"Larissa, let's work together on this. We can help you."

I knew she meant well. That was why I stood there with my hand on one rock for a moment. A finger traced each symbol that was etched into its surface. They were there, and she put them there, but they were not deep. I remembered what Mr. Demius said about the runes I used to block Jean St. Claire. They are only as strong as the witch who placed them, and it was taking nothing but my finger to rub them off the rock after just a few wipes. I did think about stopping at that point. I honestly did. I had a great level of respect and love for her, for everyone here, but I also loved Mrs. Norton and I couldn't let her suffer anymore, and I couldn't let Jean exist as a threat to myself or any of the others.

The thoughts of what I was about to do sickened me. I had to do it. There wasn't any other way. I had to go, and that meant one last show. One that would destroy someone I looked up to. Maybe even worse, I was going to obliterate the image of what she was, or what they thought she was in front of the growing audience. I pushed my hand through the rocks. At first there was a glow, and then a great crumble before they all crashed to the floor. Then I threw my own runes, not to open or lock the door, but to destroy it, so no one could follow. A great fire raged up the wall, leaving a flat wall in its place. Before she could react or attempt to counter, I turned and pointed between her and Jennifer. "Portale ora!" The spot exploded into a large disk that only I could see through. The rest just saw the thin horizon line. I rushed through and jumped, letting it close behind me after I landed on the road, landing up to a plantation house that had seen better days.

26

Time had not been kind to my home. The paint had all but peeled away in the onslaught of the breezes from the Gulf of Mexico just a few miles to my south. The hot sweltering sun of the sunbelt baked away the rest of it. The screen door all but fell off its rusted hinges when I opened it. From all appearances, it looked like no one had lived here in just over eighty years.

Inside looked like a time capsule encased under a protective coat of dust. The chairs that I remember being knocked over in the parlor during the struggle were still lying right where they fell. I stood at the bottom of the stairs looking up at where my room had been, and I guess it still was. In the kitchen, my mother's coffee cup sat on a saucer on the table. Its contents had long dried up, but a greying stain remained. A faded memory of its original purpose. Me, I stood there in this place feeling the shock of being here, the shock of what I had just done, the shock of what was happening to Mrs. Norton, and the shock of what had happened here so many years ago. The moment my life was destroyed and changed forever.

Come to think of it, I had probably just done the same with my future. Why stop there? Mrs. Saxon was right. I needed some help, but it wouldn't be the type of help she thought she could provide, but that help would also come at a price, and that would be pain that someone else I loved very dearly would have to deal with. Before I destroyed that last meaningful relationship that still existed in my life, I sent a little breeze through the house to do some cleaning and straightening up. This was going to be home for a bit. I might as well make it livable. After the last of the dust exited out the front door, I sat in the chair in the kitchen that felt strangely like it did each time I came to visit my mother where-ever that was.

I sat back and let my mind fade to that place. I didn't move, and everything stayed the same. There was no coming in through the front door and walking around this time. I was sitting right there in that chair, while my mother stirred a pot at the stove. "Hi, mom."

She jumped at the sound of my voice, and the pot of brown broth hit the floor with a loud bang and a splash. "Larissa, you gave me a fright." She reached for a towel, but I had it cleaned up and back on the stove before she turned back around. There was pride in her eyes when she saw it, but I knew that wouldn't last. Not with what I had to tell her.

"Mom, I need to tell you something. You aren't going to be happy about it, but I need you to remember that I am fine." There was no easy way to break your mother's heart, and just the thought of what I was about to do robbed me of the words. I had to force myself to do it. It was something I was going to have to do one day. I just didn't expect it to be this soon, or for this reason. I needed her help. "Mom, have a seat." I slid the chair across from me back away from the table, and she sat.

"That day," I started, sounding like nothing more than a wheeze. "That day Jean St. Claire sent his vampires after my father. They attacked you, and they attacked me. Do you remember that day?"

"Well, yes. It is a haunting memory that I try not to think about. It was a truly terrorizing day, but my one solace from that day was that you survived." The broken woman that sat across from me leaned forward and held my hand. I was her one light that made that memory bearable. Too bad I was about to snuff out that light.

"That day was eighty-three years ago." I paused to let that sink in, hoping she would make the leap on her own. For some reason, which would make it easier than if I had to say the words.

She pulled her hand back, not a reaction I expected, but I understood. Shock takes many forms. The hand that had held me was now over her mouth while her eyes stopped blinking. "Larissa, I am afraid I don't understand," she said weakly.

Dang it. I needed her to. "It's been eighty-three years since that day you and I were attacked by vampires. The day you died." There it was, or I hoped. Her eyes searched me up and down. What was she looking for? I hadn't a clue. To her, I was still the little girl she remembered. Nothing she saw would tell of my true self.

"So, how old are you now?" She asked, sitting back in her chair.

"Well, it depends. By the calendar I guess," I quickly did the math in my head, "ninety-nine years old, but physically I am sixteen." There it was, and how I expected this to go, I wasn't sure. Did I expect her to simply look across the table at me and say, "so you're a vampire"? Absolutely not. I expected an emotional reaction, but not a leap up, sending her chair spinning across the room, and before she fell to the floor sliding against the wall at the opposite end into a mass of wailing humanity.

"Mom, I'm fine!" I screamed as I rushed to her. When I attempted to wrap my arms around her, I felt her flinch, just once, but it was there. Then she gave in and fell against me while she sobbed uncontrollably. I stroked her red hair to help soothe her while I kept repeating, "Mom, I'm fine. Really." Of course, if a loved one had just told me what I let her in on, I wouldn't really believe that. So, I took the moment to tell her the rest of the story, hoping it would reassure her and bring her some comfort. I know this part comforted me.

"Mom, it's not like you think. The same vampires that killed you, the ones Jean St. Claire sent," she shuddered when she heard that name, "thought they had killed me, but they hadn't. I was still alive, barely, when two other members of their coven, the Nortons... Remember when I asked you if you knew that name?" Either she hadn't made the connection, or I didn't wait long enough for her to respond before I continued. "Well, they arrived to try to stop what was going to happen. When they found me, I was almost dead, and they turned me to keep me from dying. They then took me in and raised me as their own for a long, long time. Mom, they were so good to me, and raised me as their own. They are why I am all right now."

A lump gathered in my throat as I prepared myself to tell her the next part. "Mr. Norton," the lump got heavier and threatened to choke my voice away. I pulled my mother tighter, for my own comfort this time, not hers. "When I was turned, I was still a witch, but now I was also a vampire. When Jean found out I was both, he wanted me, or my blood, to try to become both too. They hid me from him for years. Mom, they protected me from him from that day up until just a few months ago. That was when Jean found us and sent a vampire after us. Mr. Norton fought him and died trying to protect me. Mrs. Norton, mom you would have loved her, she is so kind and loving, she... she sent me to the coven to help protect me, but he caught her and... mom he is torturing her right now. He came after me in the coven. He won't stop until he has me. I need to face him. I need to end this, and I need your help. We all do."

I felt the strength return to my mother, one muscle at a time as her body stiffened next to me. She managed to sit up on her own and sat back against the cabinet door and looked at me. To say the look was heartbroken was the understatement of the world. Devastated would be closer. The color had drained from her face, and that glint that I always saw in her blue eyes was gone, leaving them as black and empty as my own.

"Mom, I am fine. Honest," I said and grabbed her hand, holding it between both of mine.

"I know," she said, but her voice wasn't much more than a quiver as she fought back another round of sobs. "I know," she repeated, more to convince herself than to agree with me.

"I do need your help. I am here, home."

My mother looked at me and pointed down at the floor and mouthed, "here?"

"Yes. Here. In this house. I am going to need your help with what I need to do, but I think I am going to need others as well. I don't know this place, this town. Are there any families that might be still around that I can reach out to?"

She nodded. "I might know of a few."

"They can't be part of the council. I don't want them to know I am here."

She nodded again and seemed to understand.

My mother gave me four names that I was to look up, which she thought might be a difficult task. In the time that passed, there was no guarantee any descendants were still around, even if they still lived in the area. She told me I could ask around, but to be careful. People are funny about others who ask questions. Some things never changed. Of course, there was no Google back in her day. No one had to ask anyone now. You could just type in a name in the search bar and find out everything you wanted to know. A quick stop at a library or some place with a computer and I could easily check things out. Of course, I didn't even know where those places were. The prospects of exploring gave me a fright. This was Jean's backyard. There was no telling who I might run into.

That thought was resonating in my head when I heard the hinges on the screen door squeak. I had replaced the rusted ones in my effort to restore the place, but I left that, that familiar sound that I grew up with. It just wouldn't be home without it. A tremble flowed through my body as I stood up. There was none of my spring for the door ready to let loose on who ever came in through the door. Instead, I was cautious, fearful.

"Larissa?"

I heard the voice but didn't believe my own ears. It wasn't possible and had to be a trick. An attempt to lure me out and into the opening, but then I felt it. The thump-thump of several hearts. Familiar rhythms. I stepped through the door, and at the first sight I ran down the hallway and into Nathan's arms. There was no kiss, not yet. I just needed to feel his arms around me, and it appeared he needed to as well. We swayed back and forth there in the hall. Behind him, I saw Laura, Mike, Martin, Rob, Jack, and the biggest shock of all, Gwen.

I gave each a huge hug, well, all except Gwen, who appeared to think about it before backing off. When I hugged Jack, I commented, "I thought those runes would take Mrs. Saxon down longer."

"You forgot the back door, or that I could create a door anywhere." Then the last of their party walked in through the door.

"Clay?"

Up Next – Coven Cove Book 4—The Curse of the Crescent Moon

1

"Relax," Jack ordered. He had both of his hands up, ready to try to restrain me. Nathan had grabbed for my hands, but I yanked them away. The others parted like the Red Sea. Nathan made another grab, and I avoided his grasp. His arm wrapped around my waist, and I felt the taut muscles in his forearm twitch and strain as he held me back. Light glows were starting in Jack's hands. "Larissa, he is fine. He's clean. Your runes blocked Jean for good, and Mrs. Tenderschott cleaned the love spell."

Clay held his hands up, like a criminal held at gunpoint. He only wished it was just a gun pointed at him. I could do so much worse than just splatter a bit of him against the wall of the hallway, and I was cocked and read to go off. Having him, a creature under Jean's control, in this house was vile.

"Larissa, it's true. He's clean," Nathan said. The physical strain of holding me back was evident in his voice, but it still sounded sweet, and that backed me down a notch. I thought I even heard two sighs of relief as I rocked back on my heals.

"Larissa, I am fine now, and I am so sorry."

"Sorry, Clay. I have heard a few apologies from you in the past."

"Remember, you were in my head. You know what created all this. That's not me, but if you don't believe it. There is one way you can be sure." With that, Clay held out his hand. It trembled lightly, hanging there in the air. I knew what he meant and pushed Nathan's arm from my waist. Jack moved aside, and I walked slowly down the hall past the others. Each looked on fearfully.

"Stand still, or so help me god, you will end right where you stand."

"That honestly doesn't sound that bad," Clay said. The remorse in his voice pulled me through the pain of the memories he caused.

"Just stand still," I said, a little less intensely than before. I reached my hand out, but I was hesitant to make contact. I needed to know, and this would be the only way. My flat palm touched his, and there was nothing, and that was the happiest I had ever been with nothing, but I needed more. "Come here."

My fingers wrapped around Clay's hand, and I yanked him into the parlor and sat him down on the burgundy settee in front of the open window. The cool breeze of the southern winter night carried in the refreshing scent of honeysuckle. How I had missed that smell. I knew I would smell the lilac and lavender tomorrow when the sun warmed the fields, if the plants were still there. I sat next to Clay. Nathan entered the room, but the rest still seemed a little leery of these events and stayed out in the safety of the hallway. Nathan's jaw twitched nervously as he looked on.

"Relax," I said to him, and he just shoved his hands down in his pockets as hard as he could.

"Clay, I need to check something to be sure."

"You aren't going to burn any fancy letters into my skin again?" He asked, and leaned away from me cautiously.

"No. No more letters. Just another trip into your head." Clay jerked back even further away. "And no potions either."

He almost looked relieved.

What I was about to do was something I hadn't done before. I had read about it and seen my father do it probably half a dozen times. Would this work? Who knew? With only one way to find out, I placed my hands on either side of his temples and massaged my fingers back and forth. There were no words, just focus, and at the moment, that didn't seem to be a problem anymore.

Slowly the feeling of my fingers on his skin changed, but not to how it felt before. His skin stuck to mine, then my fingers sank into his skin each time I pressed. When all eight fingers sank in and my thumbs securing his head, I knew I was in. At this point, there were two options. I could either plant a thought or read a thought. My mission was to read them. In particular, I wanted to read the thoughts of who else might be in here. I could probe as deeply as I wanted to, but having been subjected to that more times than I could remember, twenty-two, and still feeling a little bit of those who did in there with me, I wasn't going to do any more than I truly needed at this time, and it didn't take long. He was alone in there. There was no one else, just Clay. A teen, who was full of emotions flashing from one extreme to the other with the moments of fear lasting longer than any of the others. This was Clay, all Clay. Before I let go, I felt one more emotion flash through and hold longer than the others, and I knew why he came.

I let go of Clay and settled back against the arm of the settee. Clay looked at me concerned, as did the others, which included a few who were only peeking around the door frame. "Okay," I said, and heard a collective exhale throughout the room.

"Larissa, I am sorry." Clay turned his head toward Nathan standing in the doorway, but before he said a word, I grabbed it and turned him back to look at me. This wasn't out of concern for what he was about to say. I was no longer worried about that. I felt the real Clay. The real Clay that appeared a few times and caused me to assess him as nice.

"Clay, you need to stop apologizing. To me. To Nathan," I winked in Nathan's direction, "to everyone. You weren't in control. And I know why you are here, or at least part of the reason." I had to consider the possibility there were other reasons hidden behind the raw emotions I felt, but those powerful emotions told me that only one mattered. "Time for revenge against those that turned you will come. I can promise you that." I slapped him on the shoulder and stood up.

"Well, everyone, welcome to my home."

The Curse of the Crescent Moon – Available as paperback on Amazon and Barnes and Noble.

Stay In Touch

Dear Reader,

Thank you for taking a chance on this book. I hope you enjoyed it. If you did, I'd be more than grateful if you could leave a review on Amazon (even if it is just a rating and a sentence or two). Every review makes a difference to an author and helps other readers discover the book.

To stay up to date on everything in the Coven Cove world, click here to join my mailing list and I will send you a **free bonus chapter** from "The Secret of the Blood Charm".

As always, thank you for reading,
David

ALSO FROM DAVID CLARK

The Miller's Crossing Series

The Origins of Miller's Crossing
Amazon US
Amazon UK

There are six known places in the world that are more "paranormal" than anywhere else. The Vatican has taken care to assign "sensitives" and "keepers" to each of those to protect the realm of the living from the realm of the dead. With the colonization of the New World, a seventh location has been found, and time for a new recruit.

William Miller is a simple farmer in the 18th century coastal town of St. Margaret's Hope Scotland. His life is ordinary and mundane, mostly. He does possess one unique skill. He sees ghosts.

A chance discovery of his special ability exposes him to an organization that needs people like him. An offer is made, he can stay an ordinary farmer, or come to the Vatican for training to join a league of "sensitives" and "keepers" to watch over and care for the areas where the realm of the living and the dead interaction. Will he turn it down, or will he accept and prove he has what it takes to become one of the true legends of their order? It is a decision that can't be made lightly, as there is a cost to pay for generations to come.

The Ghosts of Miller's Crossing
Amazon US
Amazon UK

Ghosts and demons openly wander around the small town of Miller's Crossing. Over 250 years ago, the Vatican assigned a family to be this town's "keeper" to protect the realm of the living from their "visitors". There is just one problem. Edward Meyer doesn't know that is his family, yet.

Tragedy struck Edward twice. The first robbed him of his childhood and the truth behind who and what he is. The second, cost him his wife, sending him back to Miller's Crossing to start over with his two children.

What he finds when he returns is anything but what he expected. He is thrust into a world that is shocking and mysterious, while also answering and great many questions. With the help of two old friends, he rediscovers who and what he is, but he also discovers another truth, a dark truth. The truth behind the very tragedy that took so much from him. Edward faces a choice. Stay, and take his place in what destiny had planned for him, or run, leaving it and his family's legacy behind.

The Demon of Miller's Crossing
Amazon US
Amazon UK

The people of Miller's Crossing believed the worst of the "Dark Period" they had suffered through was behind them, and life had returned to normal. Or, as normal as life can be in a place where it is normal to see ghosts walking around. What they didn't know was the evil entity that tormented them was merely lying in wait.

After a period of thirty dark years, Miller's Crossing had now enjoyed eight years of peace and calm, allowing the scars of the past to heal. What no one realizes is under the surface the evil entity that caused their pain and suffering is just waiting to rip those wounds open again. Its instrument for destruction will be an unexpected, familiar, and powerful force in the community.

The Exorcism of Miller's Crossing
Amazon US
Amazon UK

The "Dark Period" the people of Miller's Crossing suffered through before was nothing compared to life as a hostage to a malevolent demon that is after revenge. Worst of all, those assigned to protect them from such evils are not only helpless, but they are tools in the creatures plan. Extreme measures will be needed, but at what cost.

The rest of the "keepers" from the remaining 6 paranormal places in the world are called in to help free the people of Miller's Crossing from a demon that has exacted its revenge on the very family assigned to protect them. Action must be taken to avoid losing the town, and allowing the world of the dead to roam free to take over the dominion of the living. This demon took Edward's parents from him while he was a child. What will it take now?

The Jordan Blake Paranormal Mysteries

Sinful Silence (Book #1)
Amazon US

Amazon UK

He is the FBI's only paranormalist...
...She is america's favorite television medium.
Together they are more than the supernatural world bargained for.

Jordan Blake is the FBI's only paranormalist, a position that costs him more than a little credibility with the other agents. Throw in his girlfriend Megan Tolliver, the darling, and impulsive, host of the top cable paranormal show, "America's Medium", and he doesn't stand a chance of ever being taken seriously. But that doesn't stop them from turning to him when they come across something that the natural world can't explain, such as the mysterious death of a coed in Richmond Virginia. They sent Jordan up to just consult on her autopsy, but her spirit begs him to dig further. With Megan's help, they uncover a ring of evil that spreads up to the highest reaches of government, and cost several young women their lives to keep them silent. What is the old saying, dead men tell no tales? Well that is true, unless you have someone who can speak to the dead now isn't it? Together the hunt down those responsible and try to stay out of the way of their only true adversary, an entity who says he is the source of all Evil in the world.

The Dark Angel Mysteries

The Blood Dahlia (The Dark Angel Mysteries Book #1)

Amazon US

Amazon UK

Meet Lynch, he is a private detective that is a bit of a jerk. Okay, let's face it he is a big jerk who is despised by most, feared by those who cross him, and barely tolerated by those who really know him. He smokes, drinks, cusses, and could care less what anyone else thinks about him, and that is exactly how the metropolis of New Metro needs him as their protector against the supernatural scum that lurk around in the shadows. He is "The Dark Angel."

The year is 2053, and the daughters of the town's well-to-do families are disappearing without a trace. No witnesses. No evidence. No ransom notes. No leads at all until they find a few, dead and drained of all their blood by an unknown, but seemingly unnatural assailant. The only person suited for this investigation is Lynch, a surly ex-cop turned private detective with an on-again-off-again 'its complicated' girlfriend, and a secret. He can't die, he can't feel pain, and he sees the world in a way no one ever should. He sees all that is there, both natural and supernatural. His exploits have earned him the name Dark Angel among those that have crossed him. His only problem, no one told him how to truly use this *ability*. Time is running out for missing girls, and Lynch is the only one who can find and save them. Will he figure out the mystery in time and will he know what to do when he finds them?

Ghost Storm – Available Now

Amazon US

Amazon UK

There is nothing natural about this hurricane. An evil shaman unleashes a super-storm powered by an ancient Amazon spirit to enslave to humanity. Can one man realize what is important in time to protect his family from this danger?

Successful attorney Jim Preston hates living in his late father's shadow. Eager to leave his stress behind and validate his hard work, he takes his family on a lavish Florida vacation. But his plan turns to dust when a malicious shaman summons a hurricane of soul-stealing spirits.

Though his skeptical lawyer mind disbelieves at first, Jim can't ignore the warnings when the violent wraiths forge a path of destruction. But after numerous unsuccessful escape attempts, his only hope of protecting his wife and children is to confront an ancient demonic force head-on... or become its prisoner.

Can Jim prove he's worth more than a fancy house or car and stop a brutal spectral horde from killing everything he holds dear?

Game Master Series

Book One - Game Master – Game On

This fast-paced adrenaline filled series follows Robert Deluiz and his friends behind the veil of 1's and 0's and into the underbelly of the online universe where they are trapped as pawns in a sadistic game show for their very lives. Lose a challenge, and you die a horrible death to the cheers and profit of the viewers. Win them all, and you are changed forever.

Can Robert out play, outsmart, and outlast his friends to survive and be crowned Game Master?

Buy book one, Game Master: Game On and see if you have what it takes to be the Game Master.

Available now on Amazon and Kindle Unlimited

Book Two - Game Master – Playing for Keeps

The fast-paced horror for Robert and his new wife, Amy, continue. They think they have the game mastered when new players enter with their own set of rules, and they have no intention of playing fair. Motivated by anger and money, the root of all evil, these individuals devise a plan for the Robert and his friends to repay them. The price... is their lives.

Game Master Play On is a fast-paced sequel ripped from today's headlines. If you like thriller stories with a touch of realism and a stunning twist that goes back to the origins of the Game Master show itself, then you will love this entry in David Clark's dark web trilogy, Game Master.

Buy book two, Game Master: Playing for Keeps to find out if the SanSquad survives.

Available now on Amazon and Kindle Unlimited

Book Three - Game Master – Reboot

With one of their own in danger, Robert and Doug reach out to a few of the games earliest players to mount a rescue. During their efforts, Robert finds himself immersed in a Cold War battle to save their friend. Their adversary... an ex-KGB super spy, now turned arms dealer, who is considered one of the most dangerous men walking the planet. Will the skills Robert has learned playing the game help him in this real world raid? There is no trick CGI or trap doors here, the threats are all real.

Buy book three, Game Master: Reboot to read the thrilling conclusion of the Game Master series.

Available now on Amazon and Kindle Unlimited

Highway 666 Series

Book One – Highway 666

A collection of four tales straight from the depths of hell itself. These four tales will take you on a high-speed chase down Highway 666, rip your heart out, burn you in a hell, and then leave you feeling lonely and cold at the end.

Stories Include:

- Highway 666 - The fate of three teenagers hooked into a demonic ride-share.
- Till Death – A new spin on the wedding vows
- Demon Apocalypse - It is the end of days, but not how the Bible described it.
- Eternal Journey - A young girl is forever condemned to her last walk, her journey will never end

Available now on Amazon and Kindle Unlimited

Book Two – The Splurge

A collection of short stories that follows one family through a dysfunctional Holiday Season that makes the Griswold's look like a Norman Rockwell painting.

Stories included:

- Trick or Treat – The annual neighborhood Halloween decorating contest is taken a bit too far and elicits some unwilling volunteers.
- Family Dinner – When your immediate family abandons you on Thanksgiving, what do you do? Well, you dig down deep on the family tree.
- The Splurge – This is a "Purge" parody focused around the First Black Friday Sale.
- Christmas Eve Nightmare – The family finds more than a Yule log in the fireplace on Christmas Eve

Available now on Amazon and Kindle Unlimited

A big thank you to my beta reading team. Without all your feedback, books like this one would not be possible. Thank you for all your hard work.